DEATH IS ON THE MENU

LIBBY HOWARD

LIBBY HOWARD

CHAPTER 1

$\mathcal{I}$ sat on the couch, rolling quarters into little packets, my bloodhound Elvis sleeping beside me. I envied the hound his nap but as afternoon activities went, counting and packaging up coinage wasn't all that bad.

Campers needed quarters to operate the laundry machines at the campsite. It had completely slipped my mind that people would need change. I'd dropped the ball on a few other things during our first two weeks as well, but things at Reckless Camper Campground were finally starting to come together. Mom and I were getting ready to welcome our third week of guests. The roof on cabin six and the porch on cabin three were fixed. The weather was warming up now that we were at the end of April, and so far our guests had posted some very nice reviews online.

Yes, that hole in my living room ceiling was still there, but at least it was now covered by a blue plastic tarp. The tarp was unsightly, a constant reminder that Mom and I were cutting it close financially with this new business venture. Better a hole in the ceiling of the owner's house than one of the cabins where our paying guests were staying, though. I planned on getting it fixed just as soon as we had saved up a little cushion of money—a rainy-day fund in case something needed emergency repairs. Once we had that financial cushion, then I'd feel safe spending the money on the living room ceiling.

Although with our income flying out the door in expenditures, my ceiling wasn't likely to be fixed until sometime next year.

Mom walked in, the screen door making a "clap" noise as it shut behind her. Coming over to the couch, she handed me a stapled bunch of papers. "I've got our list for Thursday's confirmed arrivals. Ten of the twelve cabins are full. There are six camper trailers coming in, and we've got eight tent camping reservations. You want the good news?"

"Yes, I do," I exclaimed, thinking she'd already delivered the good news as far as I was concerned. Those reservations put us at nearly sixty percent full—twice what we'd been at the last two weeks. This meant we'd only have two cabins empty, six trailer spots empty, and twelve tent camping spots empty. For this time of year, that was amazing. The tent camping would pick up in the next couple of weeks. If I could keep the cabins and the camper sites as close to one-hundred-percent occupancy as possible, then we'd turn a profit in our first year even with the repairs and start-up expenses.

Well, we'd turn a profit as long as the mower kept running, and no more trees fell on cabin roofs, that is.

"The good news is that all of those guests—*all* of them," Mom emphasized, "are staying for the whole week. Thursday to Thursday."

I squealed, jumping up from the couch to give Mom a hug.

Our first two weeks of guests at the campground had all been long-weekenders, checking in on Thursday or Friday and leaving on Monday. Guests staying a whole week meant more money—which we desperately needed.

But it also meant we'd be frantically cleaning cabins, maintaining camping sites, and doing repairs during a tight four-hour window between check out and the next batch of guests checking in. Tuesday and Wednesday were usually the days we could come up for air, but that brief break would be ending and probably wouldn't return until late fall with the last of the foliage viewing campers.

"I was hoping to have more tent and RV reservations this week," Mom said as I took the papers from her.

"They'll pick up soon," I told her.

I'd been running ads on social media targeting back-packers as well as RV and hiker clubs on the East Coast. Mom had been the brilliant one who'd ensured we were listed on over a dozen hiking and camping apps. It had only been three weeks, but so far it looked like most of our reservations that weren't returning guests were coming from an app named BigfootingIt, followed by one named ParkNGo.

"Len's records show some walk-in tent campers this time of year," Mom explained. "Looks like people tend to make reservations in the summer, but in the spring, the camp-ground gets some last-minute guests. So I'm hoping we get a few more over the weekend."

I hoped so too.

"Think it'll be the same with the RVers?" I asked.

Mom held up their hands. "No idea. Maybe people haven't un-winterized their campers yet? It doesn't look like Len ever had a lot of guests with campers or RVs. From the last two years of reservation records, it seems like the camp-site appealed more toward people with tents, or those who wanted to rent cabins."

I grabbed the stack of papers and flipped them over to write a quick note on the back. Maybe I could hit the social media ads with some additional spend, or come up with a giveaway or special gift to encourage more RV and camper guests. We had ten spots for those folks, and I wanted those spots full this year. So many of our costs were fixed, and the only way for us to make money was to be at close to maximum capacity during the peak camping season.

Finances were a worry that had been keeping me awake at night. The expenses to run this place were more than I'd expected, even though I'd analyzed the former owner's financials in detail. We *needed* to make more money. And we had to do it without raising the camping fees, because charging more would put us out of the competitive range for the area and would only result in less reservations.

We couldn't raise rates until we had more to offer campers to justify the added costs. But we couldn't upgrade without more money. It was a vicious cycle and just thinking about money soured my previously good mood. We were working out the kinks. The guests loved staying here. But if we couldn't make this place profitable, Mom and I were destined to always live with a blue tarp covering the hole in our living room ceiling.

Or worse.

I stood, sticking the list of reservations under my arm and gathering up the rolled coins. "I'm going to drop the quarters off at the office, then take Elvis for a quick walk around the campground."

Mom gave me one of those looks that said I wasn't fooling her at all. "Sassafras Louise, you are *not* going to work today. You've already inventoried and restocked the camp store, cleaned the bath houses and the laundry, and made sure the canoes and kayaks are up on the stands and ready to rent. We're prepared for our guests who aren't going to start arriving until *tomorrow*. This is supposed to be your day off."

I wanted to reply that when you owned a business, you never really had a day off, but Mom was right. I was exhausted, and if I didn't make some time to recharge and relax, then I'd burn out. And I couldn't afford to burnout.

But we were so tight financially, and this first few months, this first year, of business was so important. We needed good reviews. We needed guests to rave about how enjoyable their vacation was here.

"I just want to make sure everything is in order for tomorrow," I explained to Mom. "Once we get everyone checked in, then I'll take some time off."

Mom shook her index finger at me. "No. Just no. I know you, and you won't take the time off. You'll come up with a million reasons why you need to be here doing this or that. Sassy, you bought this campground to fulfill a dream, not work yourself into the ground."

Mom was right, but old habits died hard. I was throwing myself into this business just as I'd done with my job in the corporate world, and that wasn't what I'd hoped for when I'd bought this place. I'd wanted a change. I'd wanted to give guests the same experience here that I'd had as a child, but I'd also wanted to recreate that experience for myself every day for the rest of my life.

My cancer diagnosis had been a terrifying wake-up call. No one expects to be confronting their mortality in their fifties and I was not ready to leave this world. There were so many things I hadn't done, so many things I'd put off as something I'd do later, when I retired.

Then one cold rainy day I sat in a doctor's office wearing a flimsy paper gown and contemplated that I might be out of time. There might not be a retirement. There might not be a future. I swore then that things would be different if I was given the miracle of more time. Seeing the sale listing for Reckless Camper Campground, the idyllic vacation spot of

5

my childhood, only a week after I'd been told I was cancer-free had seemed like a divine portent.

I'd sworn things would be different, but here I was, obsessively fixated on the business and completely ignoring the beauty and enchantment that surrounded me.

"When Austin gets here after school, he can do a quick sweep of the camp sites, and make sure the piers are clean," Mom continued. "You need to go for a hike. Or better yet, go into town, check out the stores, and have a nice lunch and a cup of coffee. Take a book with you."

My books were still packed in boxes, and I wasn't sure I wanted to read about hummingbird migration or the geological structure of the Appalachian Mountains, but there was no arguing with Mom when she was like this. And she was right. I needed a break. And a walk through town with an al fresco lunch sounded amazing.

Mom took the rolls of quarters from my hand, and pointed toward the door. With a laugh, I gave in, picking a random book off the shelves that flanked the fireplace, and grabbing Elvis's leash.

"Come on, boy. It's a nice day. We'll take a car ride and walk around the town. Then we'll sit outside The Coffee Dog where I can enjoy a cappuccino and read and you can look majestic."

My bloodhound jumped up from where he'd been snoozing on the couch, energized by the words "ride" and "walk."

Elvis called shotgun, so I hooked the seatbelt onto his harness for safety and headed to town, my hound drooling all over the leather seats and dashboard of my SUV.

Reckless had a population of about three thousand, which actually made it the second largest of the towns flanking Savage Lake. Derwood, home to the grocery and big-box stores, had nine thousand residents, where tiny Red Rock clocked in at barely a thousand. The town of Savage, our rivals in everything tourist and cultural, trailed us by only a few hundred, and from what I'd learned at last week's community meeting, they were determined to oust us from our "second-largest" status. Savage was not only recruiting new residents, but trying to pass some legislation to expand the town limits, hopefully scooping enough of the rural residents to push their numbers higher than ours. Helen Jeffries, aka The Bird, was determined Savage would not succeed.

The Bird scared me. She was a stork-like woman who I guessed to be about three hundred years old and probably a former schoolteacher—the kind of schoolteacher who rapped your knuckles with a ruler for talking in class then assigned you a ten page essay. Within days of arriving here, I'd needed to provide a plan for the coordination of campground events with the town festivals. I'd based most of it off what the former owner of the campsite, Len Trout, had done in the past, and had help from my neighbor, Lottie Sinclair. Still, The Bird had returned my plan covered in red ink, with a scathing paragraph of criticism and demand that "I submit something more acceptable within the next two days".

I hadn't worked as hard on my Master's thesis as I'd done on that revised plan. Even then, I'd received only a grudging "this will do for your first year."

Parking my SUV, I snapped the leash on Elvis, grabbed my tote, and headed down the street, twisting around to push the button on my key fob and lock the car. Nobody locked their cars in Reckless, but it was a habit that was hard to break, especially since I'd previously lived in a town with a whole lot more than three thousand residents.

It was a short walk down one side of Main Street, then back up the other side, so I stopped in a few places that would allow Elvis to accompany me inside. We stood in the lobby of the community center, looking over the bulletin board where I'd placed a few flyers for some of the campsite activities, trying to encourage the locals to participate. Some events like the sunset-on-the-dock paint-and-sip, the chili cookoff, the trail 5k, and the kite festival would be a bigger hit with a larger audience in attendance. Plus, if I could get the locals to shell out a few bucks here and there to attend fun events at the campground, it would take some of the financial pressure of the guest side of the business.

Besides, I wanted the campground to be a place the locals enjoyed coming to, not just vacationing folk with their RVs and tents.

Pulling a flyer out of my tote, I hung up the announcement for the First Annual Reckless Camper Campground Disco Mountain Bike Race, tentatively scheduled for early September. Hopefully I could get enough entries to pull this one off. I hadn't decided what the overall race winner would receive yet, so I'd kept it vague for now.

Leaving the Community Center, I checked out the specials menu at the Chat-n-Chew, then stopped in Bait and Beer to make sure Bobbi Benjamin would be coming by to stock the camp store later this afternoon.

That done, I contemplated heading to Ruby's Place for lunch, but ended up walking to The Coffee Dog instead. I tied Elvis to an iron hitching post on the brick patio, and went inside. The owner, Sierra Sanchez-Blue looked up and smiled as she saw me.

"Hey, Sassy. You here for business, or a cup of coffee and a pastry?"

"Both." I made a quick decision to forego lunch for something sweet instead, and pointed at the bear claws in the pastry case. "I'll take one of those to eat here, and a dozen of them delivered to the campground Sunday morning. They look amazing."

She beamed. "They are amazing, if I do say so myself.

Cappuccino? Whole milk with a sprinkle of cinnamon on top?"

I'd been in town less than a month and she already knew me so well.

"Yes, please. I'll sit outside. Also, can I get one of those doggie cookies for Elvis?" I watched as she put an artfully decorated dog cookie into a little bag marked with bones and the shop's signature logo.

"How are things?" I asked as she rang up my purchase.

I saw Sierra's daughter, Flora, daily as she was the one who dropped off the deliveries before heading to school. She was also the one who came by to pick up orders after her classes had finished. Like my new handyman, Austin, Flora attended Reckless High School.

Sierra rolled her eyes as she handed me my change and went to put my bear claw on a plate. "That girl of mine is gonna be the death of me. Five college acceptances. Five. All those applications and essays and application fees and you know what she does? She decides she wants to take a year off and work with me instead. Deshaun and I pushed her to at least accept one with a delayed entry, but then she tells us she doesn't know if she even wants to go to college. SAT prep, years of AP classes, all those trips to tour campuses, and now this. I'm ready to strangle the girl."

I made a sympathetic noise. "My son, Colter, had doubts as well during his senior year. He thought he could make just as much money without the degree, and honestly I'm not sure he was wrong, even though he did end up going and getting his degree. College has gotten insanely expensive, and in some fields you *can* have a wonderful career without a degree."

Sierra narrowed her eyes. "You're not helping here, Sassy."

"Sorry." I laughed. "As a woman with an MBA, I probably

don't have room to comment, but I think kids need time and space to consider their options before we shell out a hundred grand of their savings, our savings, and borrowed money to a four-year college."

Sierra grimaced. "When did universities become so expensive?"

"About fifty years ago," I drawled. I'd been paying my graduate loans off until recently myself and didn't wish that debt on any young person.

"Maybe I can convince her to be an electrician or a plumber instead," Sierra said as she handed me the plate with the bear claw. "Those vo-tech schools are a third of the price of a four year college."

"And electricians make some serious money," I added.

Sierra sighed. "I'm just worried she's going to spend the next twenty years living with her dad and me while she tries to 'find herself.' I'm all for Flora exploring her inner journey, I'd just like her to have a viable career before she's thirty."

"Flora's a smart girl," I assured her. "She'll make the right decision."

"I hope so." Sierra waved toward the door. "I'll bring your cappuccino out to you when it's ready. It'll give me an excuse to pet Elvis."

"He'll love that." I headed out the door with my bear claw and my dog's treat, finding a table before I untied Elvis and brought him over. As expected, he scarfed down his biscuit then eyed my pastry with his sad hound-eyes.

"That look doesn't work on me," I lied, pivoting my chair so I could eat without experiencing the mournful stare. It didn't help. I knew he was still watching every bite I took. Glancing over, I saw the slow tail wag, and the line of drool that accompanied his intense gaze.

"Fine." I laughed and broke off a piece of the pastry for the dog. "But that's all you're getting."

Thankfully Sierra came out then with my cappuccino and distracted Elvis long enough for me to finish my treat. As she made a fuss over the hound, I pulled the reservations lists out of my bag along with the flyers.

"Do you mind hanging a few of these up for me in the coffee shop?" I asked as Sierra gave Elvis one final ear scratch. "I'd love it if some of the locals came out for our events."

"First Annual Reckless Camper Campground Disco Mountain Bike Race," she read with a laugh. "I'd pay to watch that. How the heck are you merging disco with mountain biking? That's the weirdest thing I've ever heard of."

"I'll admit that I stole the idea from the rec center in Roanoke." I held up my hands. "It'll either flop or be a big hit."

She shook her head. "I don't get it. Do they get off their bikes and dance at stopping points on the race? Is there disco music along the route? Costume contest for the mountain bikers?"

"Yes." I laughed. "Seriously. The Roanoke one is just a mountain biking race, but I'm taking this disco thing way too far. And now I'm terrified no one will enter and I'll be stuck with fifty tiny mirrored-ball keychains, and a dozen Bee Gees posters."

"You are insane." She took a couple flyers and waved them at me. "But I like you and it's in my interest as well as the town's to make sure Reckless Camper Campground is a success, so not only will I post these up, but I'll convince my husband to enter. The man never throws anything away. I know he's got some wide-collar, pastel satin shirts somewhere in the attic."

I bounced with excitement at my potential first entry. "Deshaun mountain bikes?"

She nodded. "He's with a club. And he'll force them to

11

enter as well. What are the prizes? Besides disco-ball keychains and Bee Gees posters, that is."

"Pet rocks," I told her. "And I'm thinking of having macramé plant hangers, round lens, orange-tinted sunglasses, and fondue sets for the winners."

"Heck, I might put on a velour dress and mountain bike for a fondue set." She chuckled. "It sounds fun, Sassy. I'll do everything I can to make sure you get lots of entries."

"Thank you. I really appreciate it." My eyes actually teared up. I hadn't been here a month, but people in Reckless had been so welcoming and supportive. Sierra wasn't just a business associate, she was a friend. And I truly appreciated the loyalty of a good friend.

She waved my words away. "No problem. Enjoy your cappuccino."

Sierra went back into the shop. Elvis plopped down at my side with a sigh, and I sipped my coffee, trying to read the book I'd grabbed before leaving home. It was about tulip mania, a speculative craze in seventeenth century Holland that reminded me a lot of the Beanie Baby fever of the late '90s. Admittedly, some of the tulips in the pictures *were* really beautiful, but I couldn't imagine throwing a fortune, or even a hundred dollars at them. I set the book aside after a few chapters, but it had inspired me enough that I made a note in my scheduler to get some bulbs to plant this coming fall.

Then I picked up the reservations list Mom had given me with a twinge of guilt. I was supposed to be relaxing, but tulip mania just wasn't doing it for me, and I wanted to see who our guests were this week. Were they adults? Any families with children? How old were the kids? I'd just take a quick look, make some notes and when I got back to the campground, I could tweak the planned activities.

I needed this campground to be a success. I needed to

make sure we had enough money coming in to cover more than just our operating expenses.

The little voice in my head informed me that this was supposed to be a fun adventure, and here I was turning it into a stressful business enterprise. That voice said I should relax, enjoy my coffee and the sunshine and time with my hound, and leave all the work for later.

I hadn't bought this campground to throw myself back into the corporate sixty-hour workweek. This was supposed to be my new life, my dream. And dreams included time for friends, family and...what had Sierra called it? Self-discovery.

But as I'd always done, I ignored that voice and got to work.

CHAPTER 2

I'd just started to go over the guest list when a familiar voice called my name.

"Sassy? Fancy meeting you in town! How are things going at the campground? I was going to run by later this afternoon to see you."

It was Lottie, my next door neighbor. She'd gone from potential friend to best friend status the first week I'd arrived after she'd supplied us with food, helped me navigate the town community committees, and whacked the man who was planning on murdering me over the head with a bottle of decent red wine.

From her greeting, you would have thought we hadn't seen each other in months, but Lottie stopped by the campground every day or two to chat, gossip, bring over food, and enjoy a cup of coffee or tea. She was quirky and fun, with a big, curly, mullet hairdo straight from the eighties, brightly colored clothing, and an infectious laugh.

"Lottie! Have a seat." I motioned toward a chair as Elvis got up to greet her. A wave of guilt surged through me that I hadn't followed up on that dinner I'd planned to host for her and, hopefully, her husband who always seemed to be away on business. Lottie was the one who initiated most of our get-togethers, and I really needed to start doing my part to reciprocate.

"It's been a crazy few days," I told her. "But I think we're getting a handle on running the campground. And look at our guest list for this week!" I pushed the papers over to her. "All of them are registered for a whole week!"

"That's great." She finished petting Elvis and settled into the chair across from me. "I love what you've done with the campground. I mean, it was nice when Len was running it, but I think the activities really give it something extra."

"I hope so." I pulled out my planner. "Can you come by the bonfire on Friday? And maybe you and Scotty can come over for dinner Tuesday? I've been meaning to have you both over."

It would be a little embarrassing hosting them for dinner with the blue tarp still covering the hole in my living room ceiling, but I didn't want to keep delaying our get-together, and Lottie didn't seem to mind the currently rough state of my housing.

"Oh, I'd love to come to the bonfire and do dinner, but it's going to have to wait," she told me as she picked up the guest list. "I've got exciting news! Amanda called me yesterday to tell me she's engaged. I'm driving down tonight to spend a few days with her, helping to plan the wedding!"

I clapped my hands together. "I'm so excited for her, Lottie. And for you. Weddings are so much fun!"

She laughed. "I'm thrilled. She hasn't been dating Eric for very long, so I was totally surprised. Even though I hoped he would be the one, I didn't expect an engagement so soon."

"I'd be glad to help any way I can," I told her. "Colter and Greg did most of their own thing and I only was in charge of helping plan the reception, but I'm happy to pitch in and do research on venues or florists or caterers for Amanda's wedding."

"Well, we only plan on looking at dresses and possibly wedding venues while I'm down there this week, but I might take you up on that offer later." Lottie waved a hand. "Or not. Amanda might decide she wants to handle it all herself and all she wants Scotty and me to do is write the check. One thing having adult children has taught me is to keep my expectations low and my opinions to myself."

"I hear you there." I toasted Lottie with my cappuccino and smiled.

"Even if she decides she wants my help, the wedding will probably be…" Lottie's voice trailed off and she frowned, looking down at the list of guests. "You…you didn't rent to the Masons this year, did you?"

I pulled the papers back from her, scanning the reservations. "Yes. They come every year. We've been giving priority to previous campground guests, trying to be loyal to our return customers. Why? What's wrong with the Masons?"

The Masons were Peter, Paul, and Philip—aka Rusty—who'd been coming every April for the last three years to fish and hike. I hadn't thought twice before accepting their reservation for one of the cabins.

"Well…" Lottie eyed the door to The Coffee Dog. "They drink. Then they puke in public places. And urinate in public places. Which the town tends to tolerate to a certain extent because tourism is our bread and butter. But last year…"

Dread settled like a lump in my abdomen. "What happened last year?"

"There was an issue with one of them. The eldest one—Paul, I think. Sierra went nuts. She told the guy if he ever came back here again, she'd kill him. I figured Len must have put something in his records about it, but I guess not."

I blew out a breath, settling back in my seat while sending

a nervous glance toward the door of the coffee shop. "No, there was no note or anything that led me to believe there'd been any problems. I swear Lottie, if I had known, I wouldn't have accepted the reservation. But I saw they'd been coming for years, and figured they were valuable clients. I don't want any trouble, but they're arriving tomorrow morning. What can I do?"

Lottie grimaced. "That's not good, but it's not your fault. Maybe everything will be okay this year. It might be okay."

I heard the doubt in her voice and leaned in to whisper. "What happened? If I know, I can give them a stern warning, or keep an eye on them or something."

This was horrible. I didn't want to cancel a group of guests at the last moment like this, but I also didn't want to cause any friction between my campground and the town, and I definitely didn't want to cause any problems for Sierra.

"I don't know—and trust me, I get how unusual it is for me *not* to know something that goes on in this town. Whatever happened between them, both Sierra and that Mason guy kept tight lipped about it."

"Surely you have a guess?" I asked. "Suspicions? Anything?"

"I mean…" Lottie bit her lip and glanced at the door again. "I shouldn't say anything, not when I don't have any proof at all. I…I really don't want to gossip."

My eyebrows shot up at that because in the three weeks I'd known Lottie, she'd always been willing to gossip.

"I'm sure Sierra didn't really mean it when she said she'd kill him," Lottie continued. "She was angry and she probably didn't mean it."

"What should I do? It's too late to cancel their stay." I held up my hands. "I can't forbid them from leaving the campground. And unless there's some sort of restraining order on them, I can't keep them from going to town."

I didn't want to get a reputation for hosting rowdy guests who caused problems in the town, but I'd already accepted their reservations and I wasn't sure how to get out of this mess.

"Maybe it will all be okay," Lottie repeated. "It's been a year since whatever happened. Hopefully everyone forgot about it."

I scowled down at the reservation sheet. The three brothers were due to arrive tomorrow morning. I wasn't even sure I could get in touch with them at this point. Plus I didn't feel like I could cancel their stay at the last minute based on an incident I didn't even know the details about.

"I'll talk to Sierra about this," I said to Lottie. "Warn her that they're coming and get her side of the story."

If it was something truly horrible, I'd turn the men away. If not, then I'd see how things went this year. Perhaps they'd learned a lesson from whatever happened last year and would be on their best behavior. If not, then this would be their last vacation at Reckless Camper Campground.

Leaving Elvis with Lottie, I headed inside and set my empty coffee cup and plate in the dirty dish bin.

Sierra came out of the back as the door chime rang, smiling over at me. "Oh, you didn't have to bring those in. I would have come out to get them."

"I actually needed to talk to you a second." I gestured toward a café table with two chairs, and waited until we'd both sat down before continuing. "I accepted a reservation for the Mason brothers for this week. There weren't any notes in the reservation system about them, and they're returning customers, so I didn't think twice about okaying their stay."

Sierra took a deep breath, then slowly let it out. "Darn. I'd hoped they wouldn't come back."

"Is this a problem?" I asked. "Lottie and I were going

over the guest list and she said there had been an altercation between you and one of them. She didn't know what it was about, so I need you to let me know if I should try to cancel their reservation or turn them away when they arrive."

The other woman shook her head. "I can't do that to you. You're running a business, and had no reason to decline their request. Maybe things will be okay this year," she said, echoing Lottie's hope.

I felt a wave of relief wash over me. I disliked confrontations and was dreading the potentially ugly one I'd be facing if I had to cancel the Masons' vacation less than twenty-four hours before they were to arrive.

"Are you sure it's okay?" I pressed. "What exactly did they do?"

My mind was conjuring up the worst of crimes. Assault. Murder. Rape.

Sierra waved away the questions with an awkward laugh. "It's okay. Honestly. I don't want to go into what happened. That's all in the past, and it's not going to ever happen again."

"Lottie said they were drunk and rowdy," I continued. "I can't suddenly ban alcohol, or keep them from going into town, but I can keep an eye on the drinking and their behavior."

As much as I hated confrontation, these were tough conversations I'd absolutely have. Len Trout, the campground's previous owner, hadn't branded the business as tightly as I intended to do. We were a family-friendly place, and while I absolutely wanted people to relax and have fun, and realized for many that included alcoholic beverages, I wasn't going to let a group of guests turn my campground into a college frat party.

Sierra reached out to put her hand over mine. "This is not your problem, Sassy. I'll handle things on my end. You just run your campground and don't worry about me or about what happened last year."

I would have worried a whole lot less if I'd known what had happened, but Sierra had a right to privacy on the matter. So instead of pushing her further, I turned my hand over to grip hers.

"Okay. But if the Mason brothers cause any problems, if they're rude to you or your family, you let me know. If they're trouble, then this will be their last year at Reckless Camper Campground."

"Thanks, Sassy." She squeezed my hand and smiled. "You're a true friend. And it will all be fine. We'll keep our distance and the week will go by without incident."

CHAPTER 3

I spent the rest of the afternoon restocking the camp store, double-checking the cabins and the camper hookups, and trying to level one of the washing machines that attempted to walk right out the door every spin cycle. Austin arrived around four, after his classes were finished at Reckless High School, and I set him to mowing and weed eating, wanting those noisy activities completed while the campground was still empty of guests.

Mom and I had pushed our dinner hour to seven after discovering five o'clock was the time when every guest seemed to need us for something or another. Actually most of my dinners during the weekend tended to be a quick bite shoveled in as I managed campground events and prepped for the next morning. During the week I tried to eat real food, but I was very much aware that when guests were staying for a week or two at a time, even those meals might turn into granola-bar dinners.

Tonight 's menu was a white-bean, chicken chili that I'd put in the Crockpot this morning, and some cornbread mom had made this afternoon. My mouth watered just thinking about it.

Since the chili needed at least another hour in the pot, I took advantage of the unexpected free time. Snapping a long leash on Elvis and grabbing the book from my tote, I headed to the dock.

The book on tulip mania was as boring at the lake as it was in front of the coffee shop, so I set it aside and just enjoyed the view. The daily temperature had been edging into the lower seventies but as the sun went down, the air began to feel pleasantly cool. It wasn't hot enough yet for the mosquitos and gnats to swarm, but the low slant of the late sun felt good on my skin. A slight breeze carried the scent of freshly mown grass, and dogwood blooms. Light danced off the dark surface of the water. On impulse, I kicked off my sneakers and dangled my legs over the edge of the dock, brushing the water with my toes. It was warmer than I'd expected—only a littler cooler than the spring air caressing my skin.

Elvis stirred at my side, scrambling to his feet and turning around to whack my head with his tail. I looked up, expecting to see Mom and was surprised when my gaze met that of Jake Bailey.

The sometimes-deputy of Grant County wore jeans and a T-shirt that had seen better decades. His dark gray beard had been recently cut short, making me wonder if he purposely grew it long for winter or if his trimming schedule allowed for months of growth. He ran a hand through silver-streaked hair that was definitely in need of a more frequent trimming schedule, and grinned as he walked down the dock toward me.

"I didn't want to startle you. Was afraid you'd fall in if I called out your name or something. The lake's too cold for me to be happy about jumping in for a rescue."

I smiled back. "First, I *can* swim, you know. Second, the water's actually pretty warm. Pull off your shoes and see for yourself."

He sat beside me and immediately got a lap full of hound. "That's right. It's Elvis here who has questionable swimming skills. And I'll pass on the footbath, thanks. You northern girls might think the lake is warm in late April, but it's still too cold for me."

"Northern girls?" I laughed. "I resent that, Mr. Bailey. I grew up below the Mason Dixon line, I'll have you know. Having lived three hundred miles to the north of Reckless doesn't make me a Yankee."

"Does to me." He looked around the lake as he scratched Elvis on the chest. "I grew up in Georgia. And I'm not getting in this water until the temperature's closer to ninety degrees."

"That'll put the water temperature at close to eighty. You might be wishing for a dip in refreshing sixty-degree water come July."

He shook his head. "I like it warm. I'd love to head south for the winters, but I've got the horses to take care of. Thankfully it doesn't get really cold here, and I don't mind the snow as long as it melts in a few days."

"Melts into a muddy mess," I teased. But I actually agreed with Jake. A winter wonderland was beautiful, but a few days below freezing were more than enough for me. Thankfully, even in January, it seldom got very cold in this section of Virginia.

"Speaking of the lake, I wanted to ask a favor of you. Well, maybe not a favor because I'd be happy to pay. But it's kind of a favor, because you're practically across the road and the nearest place, so it would be really convenient for me."

I shook my head because I had no idea what Jake Bailey was talking about. It was a bit surreal seeing him so uncomfortable and even flustered, though. Jake had been a cop before his retirement, mounted police to be exact, and he exuded a confident, take-charge air that was the opposite of his current uncertainty.

"Your dock," he clarified with a charming, lopsided grin. "I don't have any water access at my place and the public launch is at the other end of town. I want to do more fishing this year, and it would be a whole lot easier to make that happen if I could put in closer to my house. I'd be happy to pay a fee, and I can work around the campground activity schedule. I'd be sure to move my truck and trailer wherever you want as well, so it's not blocking the view or anything."

"Don't be silly. Of course you can use the launch, and there's no need to pay anything. It's not like I'm using it myself." I waved a hand at the sloped ramp leading down into the water. People did walk their canoes and kayaks down the ramp, but just as many launched from the sandy area that guests also used for swimming and sunning.

He shot me a quizzical look. "Aren't you going to use the pontoon boat? Or the Bayliner?"

I assumed by Bayliner he meant the ancient sport boat I'd found under six inches of dust and mouse droppings in the garage. "I'm going to have Austin look at the pontoon boat and let me know what it needs. I think the other one might be a giant paperweight—or anchor—at this point."

He frowned. "Engine blown? Hole that needs fiberglass work? Len hadn't taken either of the boats out in the last few years, but I didn't think the Bayliner was ready for the junk heap yet."

"I really don't know," I confessed. "I don't know anything about boats and I can only afford so much for repairs. I think the pontoon boat might be cheaper to fix and of more use as far as guest activities go. Plus I'm guessing it will be easier for me to learn to drive or pilot or captain or whatever."

He chuckled, and shook his head. "Len used to take people out to get towed behind the Bayliner on inner tubes, but you're right, if you don't know anything about boats, the little pontoon is probably the better place to start. Have Austin take a look at the Bayliner though, just to see what it needs. And I'd be happy to take it out for a test drive as long as someone follows behind in case I start sinking and need a rescue."

"I'm assuming that test drive will need to wait until July when the water is warmer? Just in case you go for an unexpected swim?" I teased.

"Since you're letting me use your launch, I'll brave the cold water," he replied with a grin. "It's the least I can do. How are things going with the campground, by the way? This will be your third set of guests, right?"

"Yep. I think we've got the basics worked out, and everyone seems to like the activities I've been running. I'm a bit nervous for our busy season, though."

"You'll do fine. People are coming here to relax and enjoy nature. They're more tolerant of hiccups than if you were running a high-end ski resort in the Alps," he reassured me.

"Well, I'm dealing with one of those hiccups now." I shifted to face him. "Do you know what happened between the Mason brothers and Sierra Sanchez-Blue last year? I accepted their reservation since they were returning guests, and just now heard that there was an issue."

Jake frowned for a moment. "I remember that. I really don't know what started the whole thing. One of the Masons —the eldest one—called in a complaint that Sierra had threatened him. Sean went over to talk to her as a formality. No charges were filed or anything."

"Paul Mason complained about *her*?" I blinked in surprise that our local deputy had needed to talk to the owner of the coffee shop. "I thought *she* was the victim here, that they got drunk and vandalized her shop or something."

He shrugged. "That may have been the case. She didn't file any complaints about them with the police. Or with the campground, evidently. I'm sure if she'd have told Len, he would have kicked the guys out and made a note in the reservation system. The man was pretty meticulous about his records."

I nodded, remembering the database the former owner had put together cataloguing his extensive collection of books. "So they did something to Sierra or her business, and she threatened them—which I can absolutely see happening —then they called to complain about *her*? That's a horrible thing to do. It makes me wish I'd never accepted their reservation."

Jake shot me a sympathetic look. "People say and do a lot of things in the heat of anger, and most of them never follow through on any of it. The Mason brothers didn't know Sierra. If they were drunk and she was yelling at them and threatening to run them through her coffee grinder or something, they might have worried she was serious. Or they may just be entitled jerks who wanted to get her in trouble. Clearly everyone calmed down by the next day since there were no charges filed by either of them. The situation didn't escalate. But if I were you, I'd give Sierra a head's up so she can stay away from the campground and your guests for the next week, just to avoid any awkwardness."

"I've already spoken to Sierra about it." I rubbed the back of my neck, getting a headache before the guests in question had even arrived. "I'll have a chat with the brothers when they check in. I don't want the campground to get a reputation in town or online for having rude, drunken guests who inconvenience the locals or the other campers. If I need to kick them out, I will."

Jake reached out to pat me on the shoulder, then stood. "If you need backup, I'm just across the road and up the mountain. Although I'm sure you'll be able to handle any situation on your own. Any woman who incapacitates and duct-tapes a murderer, should be able to deal with a few drunken men."

"Are you suggesting I whack them over the head with a wine bottle and duct tape them?" I teased, not reminding him that Lottie had been the one who'd taken down the murderer a few weeks back, not me.

He chuckled. "No, I'm not suggesting that at all. If Sierra's threats got her a courtesy visit from Sean, then assaulting drunk and rowdy guests with a wine bottle might get you arrested.

I stood as well. "Arrested, maybe, but I'm sure the charges would be dropped. No one is going to believe a fifty-eight-year-old woman is a serious threat to three intoxicated young men."

He waggled a finger at me. "I'd testify. You whacked me in the shoulder with that broom two weeks ago and I still have a bruise."

"You do not." I laughed, lightly smacking his shoulder to prove the point. "Hey, I've got white bean, chicken chili in the crockpot and Mom's cornbread. Do you want to stay for dinner?"

I wasn't sure why I'd asked him. The moment I'd issued the invitation, I worried that he might take it the wrong way and think I was interested in him romantically or something. The last thing I wanted was for there to be awkwardness between me and the sometimes-deputy who lived across the road and up the mountain. But sitting here on the dock in the sunshine, having a comfortable, enjoyable conversation, made me want to prolong the evening. Jake was smart, funny, and easy to talk to. I liked him. Mom liked him.

But ugh. How embarrassing if he thought I was hitting on him by asking him to join us for dinner.

Thankfully Jake didn't seem taken aback by the invitation. He hesitated a second, then shook his head. "I've still got barn chores to do, and some burgers thawed out for the grill. Maybe next time?"

I smiled, relieved that he hadn't read anything into my request. "Next time. And you're welcome to come down for any of the Friday night bonfires as well. This week we're doing crafts with bottle caps. There's a prize for whoever's art is voted the best."

He grimaced at that. "No offense, but bottle cap crafts sounds pretty close to hell to me. Maybe I'll come down if you ever have a less Martha Stewart bonfire night."

"So, crafts are a no." I tapped my lip in thought. "Fishing contest, I'm guessing is a yes. How about the chili cookoff?"

"I'll judge the chili cookoff," he interrupted."

"Raft race? Lake triathlon? The disco mountain bike race?"

He blinked at that one. "Disco mountain bike...never mind. How about you sign me up to taste-test all the food ones, and don't sign me up for the ones that require me to train for eight weeks prior?"

Huh. Jake looked pretty fit to me, and it wasn't like I was expecting Olympic-level performances from triathlon and bike race participants. I didn't intend on participating in either event myself though, so I could respect Jake's decision.

"Taste-testing judge it is." I held out my hand and he shook it.

"Deal. Talk to you soon." He turned and headed up the dock and toward his truck that was parked by the office. Elvis and I watched him go. When he climbed into the truck, the bloodhound whined.

"I know," I told my dog. "I like him too. And I really wish he'd have stayed for dinner."

Dinner. With my mom. Which was not romantic at all. Because one could never have too many friends—especially capable, smart, funny, attractive friends that one was *not* romantically interested in.

CHAPTER 4

*R*eckless Neighbors:

　*Chipper/Shredder for sale. 13.5 HP Gasoline 4-stroke engine with electric start. Runs good. Never used to dispose of bodies no matter what Carl claims. Call Gaear Grimsrud for price and info.

　*I'm missing a package that was supposed to be delivered today. 1312 Black Hog Drive. If you got it by mistake, let me know and I'll pick it up — Bob Limner.

　— I've got your Viagra delivery, Bob. I'll drop it off this evening —with a smile! Sally Johns.

I'd been up since five thirty brewing the giant urn of coffee, doing a last-minute sweep of the cabins and camp-sites, and taking Elvis for a nice long walk around the campground and along the lake. I was glad I'd gotten an early start, because guests started arriving a good hour before the nine o'clock check-in time.

In the summer, when campsites would need to be turned-over the same day, I'd have to enforce the check-in time. But we'd been empty since the last camper had rolled out Monday at noon, so I didn't make anyone wait for their cabin or site. Actually, I was rather glad so many people had shown up early. It meant I wouldn't have a mad rush at nine o'clock with everyone coming in at the same time.

The first to check in were a young couple with their six-year-old daughter. Charlie and Adelaide Hellerman were first-time guests and this was also the first time they'd ever used their shiny-new fifth-wheel camper. Adelaide was twenty-five and slim with her long, reddish-blonde hair piled up on top of her head in a messy bun. She had a natural sort of beauty with a dusting of freckles and golden lashes framing her blue eyes. Charlie was her opposite with a stocky, muscular build, dark wavy hair, and dark eyes. The daughter, Lexi, took after her father in complexion, but had her mother's slight build. The girl's hair had been carefully braided, her matching blue and white checked shorts and blue top immaculate. I hoped they'd packed some play clothes for the girl, because camping was messy business and so were the crafts and activities I had planned for the children this week.

Lexi wandered off to explore the store while I went over the campground information with her parents. The girl's hands remained politely in her pockets as she eyed the candies and the selection of little stuffed animals I'd ordered last week.

"Why don't you pick one out, Lexi," her mother told her. "As a souvenir of our very first family camping trip."

I remembered my first camping trips—both the one when I'd been the child vacationing here, and the one where I'd introduced Colter to this very campground. Just like my husband and me, Adelaide seemed excited, while Charlie was distracted and...glum? Stressed? My husband hadn't been thrilled to go camping, and I'd found out about his affair soon after. But I didn't want to saddle my decades-old baggage on this young couple. Besides, nobody shelled out for a really nice camper like this unless they were serious about their family and their camping vacations. Maybe Charlie was stressed from work, or the drive here hauling a thirty-foot camper had been tough. Adelaide certainly was ready to enjoy her vacation, and so was Lexi, who'd skipped up to the counter clutching a stuffed chipmunk. I was betting Charlie would relax once they got their behemoth of a camper parked and hooked up.

Charlie paid for the stuffed animal, then with a smile that transformed his face, he reached down and smoothed his daughter's hair. "You my little chipmunk, Messy-Lexi?"

The girl puffed her cheeks out then laughed, hugging her father's legs. "Thank you, Daddy. I love him."

The man's expression softened. "What are you going to name him?"

"Ralph," the girl announced.

"Okay." Adelaide laughed. "Ralph it is. Let's go get our camper parked and situated, then we can go for a hike."

"Or enjoy the lake," I suggested. "The water's actually reasonably warm and there's a sandy beach area beside the dock. We also have canoes and kayaks for rent for either fishing or just exploring."

"I want a boat!" Lexi announced.

"Once we get the camper parked and leveled," her father said, that tense expression returning to his face.

"Why don't you let Lexi stay here," I offered, sensing that the first time backing their giant camper and getting it leveled might involve a lot of cursing and frustration. "She can play a game on my phone or draw, and you can come back to get her once you're set up."

Adelaide shot me a grateful look. "Thank you. I appreciate it."

"We don't let her play video games yet," Charlie said. "But

I'm sure she'd love to draw and play with Ralph while we're parking the camper."

I pulled some paper out of the printer, and set out a set of colored pencils for Lexi as her parents left. Elvis wandered over to sit beside her, his head on her lap as she drew. I watched the young couple turn their rig around, wincing a little as the camper's wheels drove a few feet through the grass and clipped a rhododendron hedge. I'd never driven anything that large, and didn't envy them trying to back that thing into their camping spot.

Three more guests arrived to check in—two for cabins and one a camper hookup. Lexi colored and sang, petted Elvis, and chatted with her new chipmunk, Ralph. An hour later Adelaide came in, and this time the woman looked just as frazzled and tense as her husband had before.

"Thank you so much for watching Lexi. Whew, that was tough." She laughed, smoothing back a loose strand of hair.

"She was no problem at all. Everything go okay?" I asked, a little worried that Charlie might have driven over the post with the power outlet—or worse, the plumbing pipe that supplied water to the campsite.

Adelaide grimaced. "It took Charlie eight tries to get the camper backed up straight into the spot. Not that I'm blaming him. We just bought it last month and this is our first time out."

I held up my hands. "You couldn't pay me enough to back that thing up. I'm impressed he managed it after eight tries."

She laughed. "Well, we're parked, unhooked from the truck, on shore power and water with the slides out. And we are *ready* for our vacation. Charlie's had a rough month, and we need this trip. We need it for our family."

We need it for our marriage was the unspoken part of that. And I completely understood. As ghosts of my own failed marriage swept through my memories, I motioned toward the café table and chairs. "Sit. You look like you could use a cup of coffee and a few moments to breathe."

She hesitated, glancing out the window toward the area where their RV was set up.

"Sometimes ten minutes apart helps everyone calm down," I commented.

I assumed their new camper purchase had been a whole lot more stress than they'd expected. Now that they were parked and set up, both she and Charlie could take a breath, and hopefully get their vacation off on the right foot.

"Okay, just a quick cup," she said as she sat at the table.

I poured us each a mug of coffee, then brought them over along with creamer and sugar packets. Then I sat down opposite her.

"We used to come here when I was a kid," I told Adelaide as I sipped my coffee. "And I brought my son here too. I love seeing families at the campground."

"Do you and your husband own the campground now?" she asked as she added a packet of sugar to her mug.

"No, we divorced a long time ago. I just bought the campground this year. My mom and I run it together."

She eyed me and I could see her doing the math to calculate how old my mother must be. "That's awesome. And I think it's sweet that you're taking care of your mother," Adelaide added.

I laughed. "It's more her taking care of me. She's in good health. Active. Lively."

Adelaide smiled. "Did she work when you were growing up? Do you have any brothers and sisters?"

I nodded. "Mom was a secretary, as she still calls the job, and a homemaker. I've got one brother, who lives out in Chicago." I smiled, remembering. "How about you?"

A peculiar expression flitted across the woman's face. "One sister. That's it. Mom is a dental hygienist. Dad is in sales at a heavy equipment rental place. He's been there for the last twenty-three years."

"What does Charlie do for a living?" I asked, thinking about the expensive camper they'd pull up in.

"Automobile sales. His dad owns three car dealerships, so he's in the family business. His mom recently passed away. It's really hit him hard. She had cancer, and I don't think he's gotten over the loss. His parents divorced when he was young, but he was always closer to his mom than he was his dad."

My breath caught at the C-word, remembering my own diagnosis and fears. It could have been me, dying and leaving my son Colton without a mother. I was so glad I'd survived, and so heartbroken that Charlie's mother hadn't.

"How about you?" I asked, trying to shake off the morbid thoughts. "Do you work outside the home?"

"Now I do." She smiled and glanced over at Lexi. "I quit my job when Charlie and I got married and stayed at home to take care of Lexi, but just recently went back to work." Her voice tightened as she mentioned work.

"Did you want to stay home?" I asked. "So many people feel pressured to return to work when the kids start school and it can be a hard transition."

I'd always worked outside the home, even when Colton had been little, but I felt sad for those who didn't feel like they had any other option.

"No, not really. I mean, I enjoyed being there when Lexi was little and it was a whole lot easier coordinating doctor's appointments, meals, and all that when I didn't have to be in an office forty hours a week, but I like work. I like doing something different and feeling like I'm contributing financially even though we really don't need the extra money with what Charlie makes. What did you do for work before you bought the campground?" she asked.

I told her about my job in marketing while we drank our coffee. She mentioned that she and Charlie had been high school sweethearts, married when they were only nineteen. We shared our parenting stories, hers far more recent than mine. I could hear how much love she had for her daughter as we chatted, and it made me yearn for grandkids of my own.

But that was up to Colter and Greg. In the meantime, I'd have to get my kid-fix with the children who stayed here on vacation.

"I should be getting back," Adelaide said, finishing her drink and standing. "Thanks for the coffee and the chat. I do feel less stressed than when I came in."

"Good." I stood as well. "We've got lots of activities on the schedule, some for kids, some for families, and some for the adults, so make sure you check the board outside each day."

"I'll do that." She turned to her daughter, who was still engrossed in her artwork. "We're set up at our campsite, Lexi. Are you ready to see your bed and our house for the next seven days?"

"Yeah!" Lexi cheered, gathering up her pictures and her new stuffed animal friend. "Thank you, ma'am," she told me, handing me one of her drawings. "This is for you."

It was a nice sketch of Elvis, only in Lexi's rendition the hound had purple and blue fur and orange eyes.

"It's lovely," I told her. "I'm going to hang it behind the register so everyone can see it. You're quite the artist!"

She beamed at the compliment, then took her mother's hand and skipped out the door, clutching her chipmunk against her chest.

Ten more guests arrived, one a woman who was hiking a series of trails up the east coast and had walked up the drive with her pack on her back and a Labrador Retriever by her side. She was my age, and I was looking forward to hearing her stories of adventure over the next week before she made her way north to the next campground. Before I realized it, the time was ten o'clock and I was completely energized from checking in our new guests.

"What did I miss?" Mom asked as she came through the front door for her shift. I liked to be here for the check-in and checkout rush and let her cover the times when most of the activity was sales from the camp store and rental of the kayaks and canoes.

"Fourteen of our reservations have already arrived." I peered out the window. "And it looks like three more are on their way."

Mom grabbed the clipboard. "I hope we've got more children this week. You've put in a lot of time on activities for kids. It's so disappointing when we only have one or two."

"So far we've got seven children," I told her. "Including an adorable little girl named Lexi. Look at the drawing she made for us."

I pointed at the colorful Elvis artwork that I'd taped to the back of our register. Having children here at the campground thrilled me. I didn't mind the noise or the mess one bit. I loved coming up with fun games and crafts for them to do during their vacation, and had more cheap little prizes than I could probably hand out in a decade.

"I'm so glad. I know you love having kids here, and so do I." Mom picked up the registration forms and leafed through them, wincing as she came to the last one. "There are four people in cabin five? Four *adults*?"

People didn't always list everyone in their party when they made their reservations. We made it clear that the cabins had one queen bed and a fold-out, but lots of people brought their own setups for babies, and some tucked their toddlers in the queen-size bed with them. We'd also had a few people scoot the furniture to the sides and inflate a mattress, bringing their occupancy up to five adults. It was a tight squeeze, but we didn't have any rules on how many people we'd allow in a cabin. The first few weeks in business had me wondering if we shouldn't put some of those rules in place, but I hated to discourage groups who were on a tight budget and so far those guests who'd made every inch of their cabin into a sleeping space hadn't caused any problems.

"Yep, four." I shrugged.

"You should charge an extra cleaning fee for more than two adults per cabin," Mom commented.

"I really don't want to do that," I explained. "Honestly two adults and two kids make more of a mess than four adults. We've got a damage deposit for any broken furniture. I don't want to start making a big deal over some spilled coffee or a pile of pizza boxes in the corner of the room."

Mom sighed. "Okay. It's your campground."

"It's *our* campground," I corrected her.

"You're the one cleaning the cabins," she pointed out. "If you're okay with it, then I'm okay with it."

I was about to tell her that Austin cleaned most of the cabins, when the sound of a vehicle coming up the drive caught my attention. I glanced out the window, a bit alarmed at the speed of the truck that was clearly disregarding the ten-mile-per-hour speed limit. The other three guests had parked in front of the office and exited their cars. They turned to watch the NASCAR event occurring on the campground driveway.

"Ten bucks says that's the Mason brothers," Mom commented.

"That's a bet I'm not taking." I handed her the clipboard. "Can you check in these guests? I'm going to have a chat with Speed Racer and his buddies."

Walking out to the porch, I smiled and greeted our other

guests as the truck spun into a parking space, spraying gravel onto the grassy divider.

"Woohoo!" a voice shouted from the driver's side. "Vacation time!"

I approached the truck, peering inside. The man at the wheel looked to be in his early-thirties—which was too old for this sort of behavior in my opinion. He had dark blond hair in a buzz cut and was clean-shaven with light blue eyes. His passenger had the same hairstyle and coloring, and appeared to be only a few years younger than the driver. The man in the backseat looked much younger, possibly in his early twenties. He had auburn hair that curled around his ears, a stray lock falling across his forehead. Embarrassed blue eyes looked at me through the window.

"Speed limit on the drive is ten miles an hour," I informed them.

The driver shrugged. "There was no one ahead of us. Can't see a reason to drive like some old lady."

Old lady. It was clear from the once-over he gave me that he'd put me in that category. I might hate confrontation, but I wouldn't be bullied by this guy.

"There are children here as well as pets and hikers. Speed limit is ten miles an hour and I expect all of our guests to be respectful of that."

"Or what?" he sneered.

"Paul," the guy in the backseat pleaded. "Let it go."

"Or what?" Paul repeated.

"Or you'll be spending your vacation at the Motel 6 off Route 18," I told him before stepping back from the truck. "I assume you are the Mason brothers? We have cabin ten all ready for you. Just go on in the camp store to check in. Make sure you get a copy of our events for the week. Enjoy your vacation."

I left them getting out of the car and walked back to the

39

owner's house to let the adrenaline wear off. Owning a business meant dealing with difficult customers, and sometimes having to refuse service, or in my case, kick people out. I didn't want to do that this week, or any week really. Hopefully my warning would set the Masons straight that this was a family campground and I wouldn't put up with any bad behavior. The younger one in the backseat seemed to get the message. Maybe he'd talk some sense into his older brothers.

Hoping that the elder Mason just needed to settle down a bit, I tried to calm down myself. A cup of hot tea and a chapter from the incredibly boring tulip mania book later and I was feeling less shaky and ready to go back out to greet our guests.

CHAPTER 5

*M*om was swamped, making me feel a little guilty for taking my short break in the house. There were three new guests at the counter, waiting to be checked in. Two other people stood in line to pay for beer, wine, and camper convenience packs. Two more people hovered at the sign-up list for tomorrow's breakfast and lunch. I could barely get in the door, squeezing by with repeated apologies as I made my way to the counter.

I took over checking guests in while Mom rang up those who were purchasing things from the camp store side of the business. The pair of us remained busy for the rest of the afternoon. I barely registered Austin coming in to get his to-do list for the day, or Mom and Elvis heading out for a dinner break. It felt like minutes later when Sierra came through the door.

"What? It's seven o'clock already? And where's Flora today? She isn't sick, is she?" I looked at the clock on the wall and winced, realizing that I'd worked straight through lunch and was starving.

"Flora's got homework," Sierra said with a grim mom-tone that I absolutely recognized. "And yes, it's seven o'clock. I'm glad to see you've got so many guests this week."

I beamed, thrilled that not only had all of our reservations arrived, but we'd had some additional tent campers and RV'ers show up as well. We might actually make enough money this week to finally pay for the repairs to the hole in my living room ceiling.

"You've got a lot of orders as well," I said, pulling the sheet off the clipboard. "Let me grab a quick cellphone pic of this, so I can input it in our computer later."

I snapped the picture and handed Sierra the sheet. Both of us looked over the orders at the same time, me thinking about which guests were ordering what, and Sierra, no doubt, thinking of what she could prepare in advance of tomorrow. Flora always dropped the delivery off around six o'clock to make sure everyone had their meals before they headed out for hiking or fishing. That meant an early morning for Sierra unless she could make the majority of the food the night before.

We'd worked together to make sure the food selections were either things that could be easily microwaved, or fresh on the shelf for a few hours before consumption. We also tried to ensure the offerings included items that would still be tasty after being jostled around a backpack for hours and possibly eaten at room temperature. The guests clearly seemed to approve, judging from the full sheet I'd just handed Sierra.

"Lots of grilled veggie and humus wraps," she commented. "And mini quiches."

"Everyone loves the grilled veggie wraps," I commented. "Me included. I always recommend them."

Sierra put some kind of spicy brown sauce on the wraps that was amazing. It was a little sour, a little sweet, and a lot of peppery all mixed together. As much as I loved her

Ruebens and her turkey-Havarti paninis, the grilled veggie wrap was my favorite.

"Then I'll send over an extra one for you to eat," she said with a smile.

My stomach growled at the thought.

"One dairy allergy, two vegans, and a gluten free," Sierra mentioned as she continued to read the list.

I squinted at the image on my phone. "The gluten-free says he has celiac disease," I added.

"I treat every gluten free order as if they have celiac disease," Sierra told me. "I don't care if it's the actual condition, a food sensitivity, or just a dietary preference. I almost lost my cousin to a peanut incident in grade school, so I'm very careful."

I nodded, appreciating that Sierra was so meticulous and professional. It was just one more thing I liked about this woman.

"How about we add a dozen muffins and a dozen bagels with the little cream cheese packets to the order," I said. "They'll keep throughout the day if I can't convince the early-morning coffee crowd to buy them."

"And speaking of coffee..." Sierra turned to look at the shelf, waving a finger as she counted the bags. "Three more dark roast and two morning blend?"

"Add six of your house blend in the small, one-pound bags to the order," I said. "I want to give them away as prizes at the bonfire tomorrow night."

"Then those will be half price." She smiled at me. "And I'll include a coupon for ten percent off any lunch order at The Coffee Dog. Hopefully that will bring some of your campers into town."

I smiled back, so thrilled that we were in synch like this, all of the town businesses working together to ensure one person's success was spread around. A rising tide lifted all boats. I absolutely believed in that philosophy and was happy Sierra felt the same.

"Anything else?" Sierra asked, looking around the camp store. "Tubs of hummus? Charcuterie? French bread loaves?"

That all sounded good, but even with the increase in campers I had to calculate how much we might be able to sell this week. Lots of our guests came with their own food and supplies, and many were frugal, not purchasing more than a cup or two of coffee during their stay. Others seemed to be happy to have us supply pretty much everything.

"Let's try three tubs of humus and four charcuterie. The French bread sounds amazing, but with the muffins and bagels, I think we're set on baked goods."

She nodded, also taking a quick picture of the order form with her cell phone before folding it and putting it in her pocket. "Sounds good. I'll see you in the morning."

She'd see me in the morning? Usually it was Sierra's daughter who did the pickups and deliveries.

I shot her a sympathetic glance. "Flora's homework is that bad?"

"Bad enough that you might not see her until next weekend." Sierra shook her head and looked heavenward. "Teenage girls. Zero stars. Do not recommend."

I laughed. "Oh, come on. Flora is wonderful."

Sierra's lips twitched upward. "She *is* wonderful. She's also a headstrong handful right now. We need to get through this year of high school, then hopefully she'll be off to college and on her way to an amazing, lucrative career. But right now, it's all about the AP chemistry class and getting her calculus grade up."

"I understand. Colter really struggled with science, too. AP chemistry came pretty close to doing him in." My son had gone on to get a business degree specializing in information technology, and had a lucrative career as an applications developer, but to this day chemistry still made him shudder.

"I'd hoped for a STEM career for Flora, but she seems to be more interested in graphic arts." Sierra laughed. "And boys, Lord help us all."

"Well, I hope to see her next week, once she gets her schoolwork in order."

"She'll definitely be back next week," Sierra promised as she headed out.

My stomach growled again, reminding me that I hadn't eaten since breakfast, so I flipped the sign on the door, locked the register and got the trash together.

With my keys in one hand and the bag of trash in the other, I locked the door to the camp store, then walked around back to toss the trash into the dumpster.

As I rounded the corner and saw Sierra and Paul Mason. She was doing that stabby thing with her index finger, clearly saying some angry things in her hushed tones. He stepped into her bending his head down as he growled a response.

"Hey!" I snapped in the exact same tone I used when I found Elvis with his head in the kitchen garbage can.

They jumped away, looking at me with guilty expressions, just as my hound always did.

"What's going on?" I asked.

"I was just leaving." Sierra shot me an apologetic glance, then glared at Paul before she turned around and hurried to her van.

Her retreat left me alone with the elder of the Mason brothers. As much as I hated confrontation, I hated coming across a near brawl behind the camp store more.

"What's going on?" I repeated, this time using my mom-voice. Paul Mason might have been thirty, but my son was his age, so I was guessing the stern, maternal demeanor would get him to actually answer my question.

"That woman is crazy, that's what's going on." He scowled. "If she doesn't stay away from me, I'm going to the police."

Not this again. From what I'd just seen, it seemed their feud had not died down as hoped. Annoyance spiked through me as I walked over and tossed the trash into the dumpster. The plan had been for Sierra to stay away from the campground and the Masons, but with Flora's home-work issue she'd be here twice a day for at least the next week. As much as I liked the owner of The Coffee Dog, I was irritated that less than twenty-four hours after his arrival, Sierra was already having a confrontation with Paul Mason. Couldn't she just ignore him? Walk on by, get in her van, and leave the campground? She'd *promised* me there wouldn't be trouble.

Maybe he'd said something she just couldn't walk away from. Maybe he'd cornered her and she hadn't had the choice to ignore him and get in her car. I didn't know what happened last year, and I didn't know what happened right now. All I did know was that I wanted everything to go smoothly this week—both with my guests and my friends and neighbors.

As much as I wanted to side with Sierra, I wasn't positive that she hadn't been the one who'd started the argument in this instance. Or in the one last year. But I *knew* Sierra. If she was angry enough at Paul Mason to poke her finger at him behind my camp store, then she had good reason.

"I'll talk to her," I told Paul as I closed the lid to the dumpster and turned to face him. "Why is she angry at you?" I asked as I took a few steps away from the dumpster.

He shook his head. "There was some stuff last year. It was nothing, just a misunderstanding, but that crazy woman won't let it go. I didn't file for a restraining order last year because we were leaving and I thought it would all blow over

46

by the time we came back. If she says one more word to me, I'm gonna do it, though. That woman's crazy."

"I'll talk to her," I repeated.

It might not do much good, but there had to be a way to keep the two of them apart for the week. One week. Just one little week, then I'd make sure Paul Mason didn't come back to my campground again.

Watching Paul stomp off toward his cabin, I wondered once more what had happened last year. And how I was going to handle this. I could talk to Sierra, but she'd already assured me that everything would be okay, that she would just avoid the Mason brothers, and here she'd been having an argument with one of them right behind the camp store. If she couldn't rein it in, then what could I do other than tell her she couldn't come to the campground this week?

But who would pick up the orders and deliver the food and supplies, especially if Flora was busy with school work? Deshaun had his own job, and Sierra didn't have any employees to send instead of her or her daughter. I could fax in the order each day—or e-mail, since nobody seemed to use fax machines anymore. I might have to drive in each morning to pick up the food and bring it back to the campground myself. It would put a serious crimp in my schedule, but if it kept the peace, then I'd just have to do it.

It was only six more days. After six days the Masons would be gone and we could all go back to normal.

CHAPTER 6

*S*ierra came through the door right at six the next morning. As soon as she set the food box down, she pulled a brown paper bag out of it and handed it to me.

"This is my apology offering," she said. "Not that a sandwich and two bear claws makes up for last night. I'm so sorry, Sassy. I promised everything would go smoothly this week, yet on the first day I can't manage to ignore that jerk and control my temper around him. I promise it won't happen again."

I was more than a little relieved at her apology. I hadn't needed to broach this tricky subject myself, and it looked like I wouldn't need to pick up the food orders this week. I'd been so worried over how I was going to manage this situation without jeopardizing either my business relationship with Sierra or our friendship that I'd barely slept last night.

I glanced at the bag with my name in Sierra's swirly script. Inside was my grilled veggie wrap, and two bear claws as well as a doggie cookie for Elvis.

"Thank you." Impulsively I reached out to hug her.

"So, we're good?" She laughed, hugging me in return before stepping back. "I take it a hug means we're good?"

"We're good." I assured her.

That settled, I helped Sierra sort through the box of orders, putting the items that required refrigeration next to the sodas where customers could easily grab their food. We'd simplified the process by allowing guests to put a credit card on file for food orders. Mom processed the billing each day, after everyone had picked up their food, and each week we'd pay Sierra for the orders minus our agreed-upon commission. It was easy for guests who just wrote down what they wanted each day on the order form, then did a grab-and-go the next morning to pick up their food. It wasn't as easy for us keeping track of who ordered what, entering it into the computer every day, and running daily charges on dozens of credit cards. Honestly, our commission probably didn't cover the administrative time, but guests loved the convenience *and* the food. And this was the sort of thing that made our campground different—hopefully the sort of thing that would see us booked throughout the season, and maybe even allow us to raise our rates a bit for next year.

Once the food orders were sorted out, I helped Sierra unload the van. She stocked the shelves with coffee while I put muffins and bagels in the covered display beside the register. So many people had ordered breakfast sandwiches that I was regretting asking Sierra for a dozen muffins and a dozen bagels. If only one or two people bought them, Mom and I would end up having to eat all of it ourselves since I didn't want to sell day-old baked goods. I needed to get a better handle on stuff like this or I'd be wasting money on food that I ended up not being able to sell.

The door jingled with the arrival of my first customer. It was Jimmy Free who was staying in cabin eight, and who I'd already nicknamed Early Fishing Guy.

Jimmy was in his mid-forties, short, thin, and balding. He exuded a calm sort of good humor with a permanent smile and an ever-present twinkle in his brown eyes. He'd talked my ear off yesterday, asking all sorts of questions about the bluegill and sunfish that I couldn't answer. He'd reserved one of our canoes for every day of his stay, so I wasn't surprised to see him this morning wearing an angler's hat and a vest that had fishing lures looped into what looked like small buttonholes. He leaned his fishing pole against the wall, set his tackle box next to it, and headed straight for the food box.

"Call me if you need anything," Sierra said to me as she headed for the door. "I'll be back tonight at seven for tomorrow's order."

I waved as she left, then watched Jimmy pull the bag with his name on the front from the food box.

"Where's Mr. Elvis?" he asked as he grabbed two bottles of water from the fridge.

"Sleeping in this morning," I joked. Elvis had gone out with me for a quick walk, but today I'd put him back in the house with Mom before coming over to the store. I wasn't sure how busy I'd be this first morning with our new guests, and didn't want Elvis getting in everyone's way and demanding pets as people were trying to get their food.

"Hope to see him this afternoon when I'm back," Jimmy commented as I rang up his waters. "I've got a soft spot for hounds. Even if the fishing's bad, I might come back next year just to visit with Elvis."

"He'd like that. Elvis never has too many friends," I replied.

Watching Jimmy grab his gear and head out, I thought about his statement. Elvis was my buddy. I loved having him by my side, but I'd been worried that guests might not feel the same love toward my slobbery hound. Perhaps instead of trying to keep Elvis out of the way, I should be capitalizing on his important partnership role in my campground. I'd been wanting to have a logo designed. Maybe I could feature Elvis on the logo just as Sierra did on her Coffee Dog logo. I could think of bloodhound-themed activities, invite the kids to play with Elvis, and make him our official campground greeter.

As the early customers came and went, I jotted down ideas. Create your own paper bloodhound mask. A sniff-and-smell contest where people had to identify certain odors. A scavenger hunt with a search-and-rescue theme. I could even get a vest for Elvis that advertised him as our official greeter. The bloodhound loved people, and especially loved children. Maybe some social media pictures of guests petting Elvis would reinforce our brand.

I was deep in thought when one of the Mason brothers came through the door, holding it open with a smile as another guest left. Looking up, I realized this was the younger brother, the one with the auburn hair who'd been embarrassed at Paul's speeding down the lane yesterday.

"Good morning, Rusty," I called out.

"Mornin', Miss Sassy," he said with a shy grin. "Just picking up our food order. Do I need to sign for it or anything?"

"Nope. Just double check the names on the bags to make sure you don't get someone else's food," I told him.

He picked the three bags from the box, then went over to look at the bags of coffee on the shelf.

"It's all freshly ground from the local coffee shop," I told him. "The bags with the red stickers are ones they roast themselves in-house."

"Is there any decaf?" he asked as he picked up one of the bags. "Peter and I drink regular, but Paul only drinks decaf and he forgot to bring some."

Drat. How could I forget to stock decaf? Just like the

rolled quarters for the laundry machines, it was something that had completely slipped my mind. My first impulse was to run over to The Coffee Dog and buy a bag for him, but I squashed that idea before I made the offer. There had to be a balance between providing a wonderful vacation for my guests and me racing around on errands when I absolutely did not have the time to do so. Mom's voice sprang from my memories, reminding me that this was supposed to be a joyful business venture, not an anxiety-ridden attempt to satisfy every guest's needs before I even knew them.

"I don't have any decaf, but I can get some in first thing tomorrow," I said instead. "Just put it on the food order, and I'll charge it to the card you have on file."

"Thanks." He returned the bag of coffee to the shelf and went over to the list I'd started for tomorrow's food orders. "I might as well write down the food we want. We've got a long hike today and I don't want to miss the deadline."

"If you get back before seven and want to change your order, just come on by," I told him, thinking I might not know exactly what I would want for lunch so far in advance.

He laughed. "We usually get the same thing every day. Roast beef and Swiss with horseradish for Paul. Turkey and hummus on whole wheat for Peter. And I get the grilled veggie wrap on lettuce with extra sauce."

"Oh, I love the grilled veggie wrap," I told him. "That's what I'm having for lunch today."

"Me too" he held up the bag. "Although half the time Paul ends up eating my sandwich. I don't know why he doesn't order a second one for himself."

Because he's a jerk who eats his youngest brother's sandwiches? I thought, a little uncharitably.

The door chimed and I looked over to see Lexi skipping in, her chipmunk Ralph in one hand. Her father walked in behind her, glancing at Rusty before following his daughter to the fridge. Rusty finished filling out his order and left. Charlie glanced at him again as he left, then went over to look at the box that now only held two bags of food.

Lexi pulled a chocolate milk from the fridge, then came over to look at the muffins by the register.

"Daddy, can I have one?" she asked, pointing at the muffins.

"Huh?" Charlie turned away from the box. "Sure, Lexi."

He went to look at the menu and sign-up list while I removed Lexi's choice of muffin from the display with a set of tongs and slipped it into a bag.

"Feel free to take one of the menus," I told Charlie as I handed Lexi her muffin. "Food orders are due no later than seven o'clock each night. Deliveries are at six in the morning. You can grab your food any time between six and noon."

He picked up one of the menus and looked it over. "And they're in this box? We take the bag with our name on it?"

"We charge the order to the credit card you have on file with us," I explained. "So there's no need to pay for the food when you pick it up. You just grab-and-go."

"And my name will be on the bag," he commented, as he looked at the two remaining orders in the box."

"Yes, and thankfully Sierra's handwriting is pretty clear. We haven't had any mix-ups so far." Although now that we were starting to get busy, that was something I'd probably need to plan against. "Any orders that require refrigeration are kept there in the fridge next to the milk and sodas, but most of the food bags are in the box."

"I think maybe I'll go ahead and order something for tomorrow's lunch," he mused, heading back to the clipboard with the form. "Do you want me to order a sandwich for you, Lexi?"

"Can I have a muffin for lunch instead?" The girl asked, looking once more at the display case.

"No, you cannot have a muffin for lunch." Charlie wrote on the form. "I'll get you a ham and Swiss with lettuce and tomato."

The girl scrunched up her face but didn't protest. With quick longing-filled glance at the display case, she turned to me. "Is Elvis here? Can I play with him this afternoon? Does he have toys?"

"Elvis is sleeping in this morning but will be here soon," I told her. "And I'm sure he'd love to play with you. He has a big tennis ball that is his favorite toy. He'll play fetch for hours with that ball."

"Daddy, can I play fetch with Elvis this morning?" she asked.

Charlie finished writing down his order and came over to the register, pulling cash from his pocket for the chocolate milk and the muffin. "We rented a canoe for today, remember?" he said as he handed me the cash. "Maybe tonight, after dinner. If Elvis is available, that is."

I gave him his change. "I'm sure Elvis will be free after dinner for a game of fetch. And don't forget the bonfire tonight. We've got crafts for the kids and the adults, and there will be prizes. We'll also have free hot cider for everyone—nonalcoholic, of course, although if you want to put a splash of something in your cup, that's fine as well."

"Sounds fun." He reached down and ruffled Lexi's hair. "Come on, kiddo. Let's go wake your mom up. That canoe isn't going to wait forever."

She laughed, the skipped toward the door ahead of her father. "Goodbye, Miss Sassy. Tell Elvis I'll see him later!"

"I will," I promised.

A few other campers came in after they left, including the two people who'd still needed to retrieve their food orders. I was just tidying up when Mom arrived, Elvis by her side.

"Someone has a playdate," I said, reaching down to pat the hound.

"Me? Please let it be me," Mom said, handing me the leash.

"Sorry, it's Elvis." I knelt down to the hound's level. "Lexi wants to play fetch with you this afternoon, buddy. With your ball. Wanna play with your ball?"

The bloodhound's long ears lifted and angled forward at that magic word. Elvis adored his ball. He also adored ripping all the yellow fuzz from it, then chewing it apart to get at the squeaker. I worried that he might end up at the doggie emergency room with bits of ball lodged in his digestive system, so I'd begun taking the toy away from him and hiding it when we weren't actively playing fetch.

"So what did I miss?" Mom asked, looking around the shop. "Besides you organizing playdates for Elvis, that is."

"Lots of boat rentals, lots of interest in the food orders, and lots of trail mix sales." I glanced over at the display case. "And not as many people buying muffins and bagels as I'd hoped."

"It looks like you sold a few of them," Mom commented.

"If it was up to Lexi, we would be sold out on muffins and chocolate milk." I laughed, remembering the girl's request to have muffins for lunch. "Unfortunately I think we're going to be the ones eating these. I over ordered, and now we're stuck with ten muffins and six bagels."

"That little girl is adorable," Mom said as she checked the fridge. "She reminds me of you when you were that age. Hmm, it also looks like we need to restock the drinks. And by that, I mean *I'll* be restocking the fridge. You've been up since five and I know you didn't sleep well last night. Go back to the house and take a nap."

I sighed, suddenly feeling every bit of my restless night. "I was worried about having to talk to Sierra about last night.

Turns out I didn't need to worry at all. She apologized before she had both feet in the door. Even brought me some goodies as a gift."

"She's a good person, and a good friend," Mom agreed. "Now go. Nap."

I held up both hands and laughed. "Okay, okay. Let me just take Elvis for a quick walk around the campground. He needs the exercise and it'll give me a chance to say hi to the guests I haven't seen yet this morning. After that, I promise I'll go back to the house and take a nap."

It was going to be a long night with the bonfire and the crafts and the contest, and I needed to be rested. There were still a million things to do, but none of them would get done if I spent the day exhausted from lack of sleep. I did need a nap, and that was one promise I was determined to keep.

CHAPTER 7

*P*aul Mason let out a whoop that I was pretty sure could be heard three counties over. The man and his brothers had arrived at the bonfire, each with a box of beer and a lawn chair, then had begun their festivities by chugging "brewskies" and shouting incoherently about something they'd seen or done that was hilarious—hilarious only to them.

I'd tried to ignore them, focusing on my other guests and getting craft participants set up with their supplies, but when Paul decided to dance around the fire pit with an empty box of beer on his head, his shirt off and some sort of blue paint smeared across his chest and under his eyes, I figured it was time I put on my big-girl panties and intervene before the rest of his clothing came off—or he fell in the fire.

Glancing at their remaining boxes of beer, I wondered if slipping a couple of Xanax in each can would do the trick. It probably would. It would also be unethical, against the law, and the completely wrong way to deal with this situation.

"Grown men acting like idiots," I grumbled as I made my way over to the three.

Deciding I'd have better luck talking to the two older men, even if one of them was dancing around half-naked in some *Braveheart* reenactment, I headed toward Peter and Paul. Rusty, the younger one, saw me coming and shoved his beer behind his back, as if *that* was going to help the situation.

"Paul. Peter." I nodded to each of them in turn, then glanced down at the boxes of beer cans. "We allow alcohol consumption, but we are a family-friendly campground. I can't have guests disturbing others with their drunken, rowdy behavior."

"It wasn't me that peed on that guy's tent," Paul quickly said before dancing away and leaving me with his two younger brothers.

My eyes nearly bugged right out of their sockets. No one had complained about anyone peeing on their tent—at least not to me. Maybe Mom had taken care of the situation and forgotten to tell me about it? That or the tent camper had just figured it was an animal that had marked his tent. Whether Paul had done it because he was drunk and couldn't tell a tent from a tree from the actual restrooms in the campground, or he'd had a grudge with the tent camper, I didn't know. And I didn't care.

"We're not drunk," Rusty informed me with a nervous smile, drawing my internal musings from tent-peeing back to the current situation.

I pointed at Paul—the one half-naked and covered in blue paint.

"Okay. *He's* drunk," Rusty admitted.

"Get your brother and hose him off in a cold shower," I instructed the two, hoping I didn't see any of that blue paint on the bedsheets when they checked out on Thursday. Six more days. And then they'd be gone and I'd never rent to these three brothers again.

Although, to be fair, the youngest one hadn't been so bad. And in the last three weeks, I'd had to deal with complaints about other campers as well. Babies screaming in the middle of the night. Loud children racing through other people's camp spots. People cooking food that nearby campers considered "stinky." Campers who noisily tromped around in the early morning hours. Running a campground was in some ways a lot like my old corporate job. I'd expected the event planning and marketing portion to be similar, but the whole managing expectations, and calming tempers thing? It absolutely was similar to having a dozen sales managers, all wanting me to do different things for them *right now*.

"Keep the beer in your cabin aside from a can or two," I said to the two men not dancing around the fire. "And tell your brother to keep the rest of his clothing on. And keep the noise down. Please."

I'd added the last, because I wanted to be polite, even though right now it pained me to say the word.

"Paul!" Peter shouted, clearly not registering my last request. "You're scaring the little kids. Put the dad-bod away and let's go back to the cabin."

Paul stopped and stared at his brother, his eyes not really focusing anywhere in particular. He swayed, and for a second I thought he *was* going to topple into the fire.

"I'm a pagan," he shouted back.

I blinked, not sure if I'd heard the slurred words correctly or not. "You all are with a motorcycle club?" I asked the more sober two brothers.

"Nah." Peter shook his head. "He means the religious sort of pagans."

"Oh." I looked back at Paul, unsure if my kicking him out of the Friday bonfire would constitute some sort of religious discrimination or not.

Rusty snorted. "We're Baptist. Paul's only a pagan when he's drunk. Idiot."

Good. Then there was no need for any religious accommodation.

"Come on, Paul!" Peter shouted once more. "I've got Fireball back in the cabin. And cigars."

"No smoking in the cabin," I hurriedly reminded them, knowing full well that I'd have to seriously air out cabin ten Thursday after check out. I made a mental note to order more Febreze.

"Just keep the noise down." I sighed, knowing there was a good chance I'd need to go over there and shush them at least three more times tonight. Maybe I'd get lucky and they'd drink so much Fireball they passed out.

I watched the three stumble off to their cabin then went back to the other side of the fire and my less-drunk guests.

"Good riddance," my mom muttered. She was sitting in one of the camp chairs, her feet up on another. Elvis, snoozed by her side. For a brief second I envied them, desperately wanting to put my feet up and relax as well. But Mom was eighty-five and had been manning the camp store and registration desk since ten this morning.

And Elvis…well, Elvis was a hound. They slept a lot. When they weren't sniffing everywhere, or slinging drool onto the walls and ceiling, or jumping up on the counters to eat that banana nut muffin you'd really wanted to have for breakfast the next day.

With a wistful glance at the chair beside Mom, I turned my attention to the rest of tonight's bonfire attendees. There was a camp potluck and cooking contest on the schedule for tomorrow, with judging by the guests and a prize for the winner, but Friday had somehow become craft night in addition to the bonfire. That first week I'd noticed it hadn't been just the kids decorating eggs and clay pots on Friday night.

Since adults wanted to participate, I'd devised complementary activities. Tonight's was beer cap art.

The children were busy gluing sticks, nuts and seeds to their boards in whatever animal shape they'd chosen to trace on the flat, sanded, piece of pine. It had been easy to find stencils for the local wildlife—a hawk, a bear, a fish, a snake, a bobcat, and a raccoon. The winner got a giant chocolate chip cookie. Of course, every child was a winner with each of them going home with a tasty treat of a prize.

I made my way among the children, pausing to compliment their artwork, then went over to where most of the adults were clustered.

They were gluing beer caps onto their slabs of wood instead of the sticks, nuts, and seeds. Same pine plank. Same stencils. But they had glue that was a bit more industrial strength to hold the beer caps in place. For the last three weeks I'd been collecting the beer caps from bars around town. I'd even braved the notorious Twelve Gauge bar. On a Wednesday. At five o'clock, right when they'd opened. The place had been empty except for the bar staff, so I'd made my request for them to save caps for me and gotten the heck out of there. I'd put up a sign at the Bait and Beer. I'd asked the staff at the Chat n Chew to save them for me. I'd even put a plea out on our Reckless Neighbors app, requesting that people drop their caps into a box I'd set up at the Community Center.

The results had been surprising. I had no idea the quantity of bottled beer that the residents of this town drank. It was a little disturbing, to be honest, although I suppose some people might have been saving the caps for their own art projects. I had way more beer caps than I needed for tonight's activity. Way more. It probably wouldn't be appropriate for me to use them in children's crafts, but maybe I could devise something else for the adults to do with them next week. Concrete stepping stones with beer caps, maybe? Although carting home a heavy concrete stepping stone from a camping vacation didn't seem ideal.

"Oh, I like that!" I exclaimed as I knelt down and eyed Adelaide's artwork. The woman had decided to do a trout, and she'd carefully chosen beer caps that would recreate the colors of the fish.

"Thanks." She smiled up at me. "I was inspired after spending most of the day trying to catch fish and failing."

I made a sympathetic noise. "Are you all renting a canoe again tomorrow? Maybe you'll have better luck next time."

She sighed. "I'm not much into fishing, and Lexi is really too young for it. She was bored after the first hour. I'm not sure we can get her into the boat even if we bribed her with muffins. Charlie may go out, though. Tomorrow I just want to relax or maybe take Lexi for a short hike."

"You're always welcome to bring her by the camp store to play with Elvis," I suggested. "He really loved playing fetch with her this evening."

"Maybe. I know she'd love that, but Charlie wants us to do family things on this vacation." Adelaide glanced once more over toward Charlie. "He was upset that Lexi was so fidgety on the boat today, but I don't know what he expected. A six-year-old isn't going to want to be in a canoe for four hours with nothing to do but stare at a fishing line in the water."

"Fishing isn't for everyone," I told her, thinking that it wasn't a sport that really appealed to me either, although I'd be willing to give it another try.

Adelaide sighed. "He hasn't been the same since his mother died, and me going back to work didn't seem to help. We needed this vacation. I was so thrilled when he bought the RV and made the arrangements, even though it was a bit last minute. But instead of relaxing he's just...angry. Short tempered. With me as well as with Lexi."

"I'm sorry," I replied. It wasn't my place to give marital advice. I really didn't know this family, or what might be going on behind the scenes. Maybe Charlie was struggling with his grief over losing his mother. Maybe he was upset over Adelaide returning to work, but didn't know how to voice his worries without sounding like a jerk. Maybe there were other problems between him and Adelaide that this camping trip was supposed to miraculously solve.

Maybe the fish just weren't biting. I didn't know.

Adelaide forced a smile. "It'll be okay. I'm sure whatever is bothering him will pass, and it'll all go back to normal. Meanwhile we'll hike or try to fish again, or do whatever family stuff he's got planned for us."

I winced at the exhaustion in her tone. "There's the camp-fire potluck and cooking contest tomorrow night. And Austin is running a nature camp for the kids at noon. They'll learn to identify plants and animal footprints, then plant some flower seeds to take home. Maybe Lexi would like that, and it would give you and Charlie an hour to yourselves."

She smiled over at me, then focused back on her bottle cap artwork. "That's a good idea. Maybe we'll do that."

I left Adelaide and made my way around the rest of the campers, then back to where Mom was half dozing in her chair. Sitting down beside her, I pulled a soda out of the cooler and popped it open.

She blinked at the sound, turning to face me. "Goodness, I think I might have fallen asleep for a moment there."

"Just a moment," I reassured her. "Here's what I'm thinking as far as the winners of our contest. All the kids are getting a cookie. For the adults, the top three are Adelaide, Monty, and Sarah. You pick the winner. All ten will get a one pound bag of dark roast, and the top three winners will also get a free day-old bagel with cream cheese tomorrow morning. Don't judge me. We've got a ton of muffins and bagels and we can't eat them all ourselves."

Mom nodded. "No judgement here. I totally approve of pawning off day-old pastries on the winners. But tell me, why am *I* judging this thing?"

"Because I need to go check and make sure the Mason brothers aren't dead of alcohol poisoning. Or wandering around peeing on tents," I informed her.

She wrinkled her nose. "That's probably a good idea. I'll try to stay awake long enough to judge this contest, but I'm not promising anything. If you get back here and I'm sawing logs in this chair, it'll be up to you to hand out the prizes."

"I'll make it quick," I promised. "Drink a Coke or something just so you can stay awake enough to make sure no one falls in the fire, and I'll be back in time to announce the winners."

"Like I can do anything besides scream if someone falls in the fire," she drawled. "And you know I can't have caffeine after three or I'll be up all night. But I'll do the best I can to keep my eyes open."

It was the most I could ask. At the last minute, I decided it might be a good idea to bring Elvis with me, so I woke the hound up and untied his leash from the chair. He yawned, then shook his whole body and looked up at me with his droopy eyes. He was tired too, but he wasn't anywhere near Mom's age in dog years, so I didn't feel bad about making him come along.

Elvis trotted by my side as we headed down the line of cabins. I didn't really think I'd need protection against the Mason brothers, but after what had happened last month, I liked having Elvis with me after dark.

My handyman had been murdered, right in cabin three. Yes, he'd been killed before we'd arrived—probably before we'd even signed the purchase documents earlier that day. Still, it was unsettling to think a violent crime had occurred at my campground not quite a month ago. Even more disturbing was that the murderer had returned several times and prowled around the property, trespassing in the cabins.

Most disturbing of all, he'd been in our house and had threatened to kill me if I didn't give him what he was looking for. I'd been lucky, and Lottie had come along at just the right time. The whole thing had ended with the murderer in jail, and me in one piece, but I was still anxious about it all. I made sure I kept the house locked up, carried a little can of pepper spray in my pocket when I walked around at night, and took Elvis with me if I ever needed to go somewhere by myself after dark.

The Masons' cabin was lit up, the orange glow through the windows a sharp contrast to the dark woods behind it. I could hear voices through the thick log walls—voices that sounded as if they were arguing rather than partying. They weren't so loud that I thought they'd disturb the other campers, but given the amount of alcohol I suspected they'd drank, I worried the argument might become a screaming match—or might turn physical. I really didn't need my cabin furniture smashed up, or guests having a brawl in my campground, so I headed for the little porch and the cabin door.

"It was her fault. She initiated the whole thing, and I'm not a guy to say no." The voice faded as if the speaker had walked to the back of the cabin.

I knocked on the door and the loud conversation abruptly ceased. The door opened and a face peered out. Rusty. The youngest of the brothers and the one who'd appeared the most sober at the bonfire.

"I'm so sorry." He grimaced. "Are we disturbing anyone? I'll try to keep everyone quiet."

"I just came by to check on you all," I told him. "No one's

complained, but you might want to keep it down a bit. People are going to start heading to bed soon."

"We will. I promise." He slipped out onto the porch, shutting the door behind him. "I wanted to apologize for earlier —for the bonfire. We're not normally like this, but it's been a rough year. Family stuff, you know? I promise things will be better tomorrow."

Better tomorrow. Like I'd never heard that before.

"No frat-boy antics in the community areas," I warned Rusty, my voice firm. "No half-naked, drunken dancing around fires or anywhere. Keep the booze within social limits, and keep your voices down. And for the love of all that's holy, no more peeing on tents."

Rusty nodded solemnly and raised his hand. "I swear."

I blew out a breath. "Good. Now get some sleep. And come by the camp store tomorrow morning for your food order and that bag of coffee."

Heaven knows they'd need the coffee. I wasn't sure I had enough coffee to help mitigate the hangover these men were going to have come morning. Besides, they'd ordered decaf, and *that* certainly wasn't going to help them get going after all they drank tonight.

"Will do." Rusty gave me a charming grin. "Thank you, Miss Sassy. And have a good night."

"You too."

Elvis and I stepped off the porch and headed back to the bonfire. Mom was still awake when we returned—barely. I announced the winners, awarded the prizes, and congratulated all the participants. Mom shuffled off to bed. Everyone stayed to chat for another twenty minutes, then headed off to their cabins and campsites. I remained behind to help Austin clean up and put out the fire, making sure all the coals were smothered and doused before we called it a night. I walked my young employee to his truck, told him I'd see him in the morning, and watched him drive off.

Then Elvis and I headed back to our house and to bed. I slept like a rock. There were no complaints of noise or bad behavior. I woke at dawn feeling refreshed and optimistic that I wouldn't have to deal with any further problems from the Mason brothers.

CHAPTER 8

$\mathcal{I}$ was up before the sun as usual, taking Elvis for a quick walk and enjoying the peace of the campground pre-dawn before heading over to the camp store. There was something magical about the colorful tents muted gray in the dark and lit only by the faint glow of the campground lights. A few of the cabins and campers showed signs of life, but everything was quiet. It made me feel strangely maternal to know my guests were safely asleep and would soon be rising to begin another amazing vacation day.

Hooking Elvis's lead far enough behind the register that he wouldn't be in the way, but with enough slack in his leash for him to watch and greet visitors, I began my ritual of coffee-making and prepping for the day. Three campers came through the door right at six in the morning, just as I was getting Elvis his breakfast.

One camper headed for the coffee, one made a beeline for the fridge that held the containers of bait, and the other went through yesterday's pastries that I'd decided to sell at a discount rather than try to eat myself.

"Sierra will be here any minute with the food orders," I

said as the woman picked up a cellophane-wrapped muffin and eyed it. Sierra usually showed up before any of the campers were stirring, but it was clear these three were getting an early start to their day. The early bird catches the worm—or the fish, I thought as I watched the one camper pull a pint of bait from the fridge.

"I'm doing the lake-lap trail today," the woman said as she handed me the muffin to ring up. As an afterthought she added two packages of deer jerky and a granola bar.

Tamara Boone. Backpacker hiking up the east coast from campsite to campsite with her dog. Staying at tent site number eight, I thought, happy that I'd remembered her from check-in.

"Whew, that's a long hike, Tamara," I commented as I scanned her purchases. "Lake-lap trail" was a bit of a misnomer. Savage lake was forty miles in circumference, but the trail cut almost half of that off by diverting onto bridges that crossed some of the outer edges of the lake. Still, twenty miles was a serious distance.

She nodded. "I did a fifteen miler yesterday, so I don't think this will be too much of a stretch."

"When do you think you'll be returning to the camp-ground?" I asked.

It was a rocky hike on fairly ungroomed trails and I didn't know how fast the woman hiked. She definitely was fit and experienced enough to handle the hike, but I made a quick mental note to check in later today and make sure she made it back okay.

She grinned, giving me a twenty and stuffing her purchases in her backpack. "If I'm not back in time for the campfire potluck, send the national guard after me."

I handed over her change, glad she hadn't taken my concern as any sort of doubt on her ability.

"You don't want to miss that," I told her. "Mom's making her famous mac and cheese."

"Then I'll be here if I have to cut my hike short and call an Uber to bring me home," she joked.

Tamara left after giving Elvis a quick pat. The man getting coffee paid and then headed out, mumbling something about going back to sleep. The man getting bait approached me.

Monty Black. One of the beer cap art winners from last night. Cabin two.

"Crickets or nightcrawlers?" Monty asked, holding up a container in each hand.

Heck if I knew. It was probably something I needed to research, given that Mom and I now owned a campground bordering a lake where fishing was one of the top three local sports.

"You can't go wrong with worms, but the woman who runs the bait store uses minnows when she's going for trout," I threw out the only piece of fishing knowledge I had.

He stared at the containers with a thoughtful expression on his face.

"I'm going for whatever I can hook on my line." He laughed, then set down the container with the worms, pivoting to take the other back to the fridge. "I'm glad those guys from last night quieted down. After their show at the bonfire, I was worried I'd be up all night and sleep through the morning."

I winced. "You can hear them all the way in cabin two?"

Cabin two in the cluster of buildings on the other side of the owner's house from where the Masons were staying. If he'd been hearing them at night, then surely I would have heard them as well.

"No, not unless they're heading to the bathroom for a pee. They don't walk or talk quiet, and they travel in a group, like noisy buffalo. But they were drinking so much last night I wasn't sure what would happen." He shook his head, a rueful smile curling up one corner of his mouth. "I shouldn't be so grumpy about it. I was young once and liked to party. Probably did the same sort of embarrassing things back in my day."

"But you're here to fish." I rang up his bait. "And it's hard to be up at six in the morning if you've been up all night listening to people who sound like a herd of noisy buffalo."

"I was actually up at four thirty." He chuckled. "I thought about walking over to their cabin and making a bunch of noise, knowing they'd be hungover and wanting their sleep, but I didn't want to disturb any of the other campers. Besides, I think at least one of them was up just as early as me."

Ugh. I hoped whoever it was just got up early and wasn't sick. Maybe it had been Paul. He certainly had been far more drunk than the others. We were only on day three of their stay here. Ugh, would it get worse? I hoped last night would be their only big bender, and they'd settle down because I didn't think I could take "worse."

Monty paid and headed out with his bait. No sooner had he left than I saw the Coffee Dog van pull alongside the camp store.

"Sorry I'm a little late," Sierra announced as she ran in, a giant box filling her arms.

"No problem. We haven't had our morning rush yet. It's just been a couple of the people going out early to hike and fish." I took the box from her and began sorting through the food orders for the ones marked as needing refrigeration while she went back to the van.

The pair of us fell into a routine, Sierra stocking the shelves with fresh ground coffee, while I put a handful of bags into the fridge and tried to arrange the others in some semblance of order. The box was full and the fragrance of fresh bread and sandwiches made me wish I'd had more than a day-old muffin for breakfast.

"We're going to need a second box if we start getting any more orders," she commented.

"Plan on it. Everyone loves the food and the convenience. Plus, you make the best sandwiches," I told her.

Sierra grabbed yesterday's box and paused by the door. "I just want to thank you again for this opportunity. The Coffee Dog has always done well, but this partnership has really taken my business to the next level. I'm planning on hiring staff, and we're starting to get some catering orders as well. I really appreciate you reaching out to partner with me. And I appreciate you as a friend."

I smiled, tearing up a bit at her words. "We do make wonderful partners. And wonderful friends."

With a wave, Sierra said she'd see me at seven for tomorrow's orders and headed out. Her van had no sooner vanished down the drive than our morning rush began. Coffee and pastries were flying off the shelves. People began to pull their canoes and kayaks into the lake, fishing poles in hand. Others headed into the woods with day packs on their backs. A couple of campers were grabbing their pre-ordered lunches before driving to other trails, the marina, the adventure center, or the avian rescue. We had six trails that cut through our campground, but Reckless and the Savage Lake area had dozens more as well as enough outdoor activities to make even the most adventurous camper happy.

And if it rained, there was always the bowling alley and the arcade in town.

The second carafe of coffee had just finished brewing when Lexi came skipping in the door, her father behind her.

I smiled over at them. "Good morning! Is Adelaide sleeping in?"

He shrugged. "She's not much of an early riser. Lexi, *one* muffin and *one* chocolate milk," he added as the girl eyed the day-old selection.

"They're half off," I said, crossing my fingers and hoping that would convince him to buy her two.

Lexi took her time selecting her muffin while her father wandered over to the food box and began sorting through the bags. He pulled a few out, setting them on the other side of the box as he continued to search. Lexi decided on her muffin and went over to the fridge, her expression dismayed.

"There's no chocolate milk!" she exclaimed.

How could there be no chocolate milk? Mom had just stocked the fridge yesterday. Had there been a run on chocolate milk after dinner when I'd been busy getting things ready for the bonfire and crafts?

Charlie looked up from the box of food. "Do you have any in the back? Is there a walk-in where you keep extra supplies?"

"I'll go see," I said, locking the register and giving Elvis a quick pat as I came around from behind the counter. "You stay here boy. I'll be right back."

I would have worried leaving the store unattended while I went into the back, but I didn't expect Charlie or Lexi to steal anything. Not that there was much to steal with the register locked and Charlie didn't seem like the type to run out the door with a shoplifted six-pack of beer.

The back room was full of boxes holding extra camper convenience packs, snacks, sodas, and beer, but we did have an old fridge we used to store our own lunches as well as extra milks and juices. I was relieved to find three bottles of chocolate milk, but still perplexed that we'd somehow managed to go through a dozen bottles in three days. Who in the heck was drinking all the chocolate milk?

"Got some!" I announced as I exited the storeroom.

I put two in the fridge, then walked over to hand Lexi the third. She was standing by her father, still clutching her muffin as Charlie still sorted through the paper bags of food.

"Did you find yours?" I asked, worried that his order had been forgotten or somehow mixed up.

"Yes." He laughed. "It was behind a bunch of others so it took me a while. And I wanted to check to make sure the order was correct."

"Was it? Correct, I mean?" I held my breath, hoping that we hadn't gotten his first food order wrong.

"Perfect." He held up the bags. "Smells amazing. Come on, Lexi. Let me pay for your stuff so we can go back and I can eat my breakfast."

I rang up the girl's muffin, and chocolate milk, wished them a good day, and watched them leave, hoping that the family had resolved whatever problems they were dealing with and enjoyed their day.

Rusty Mason wandered in not long after Lexi and Charlie had left and made his way over to the box of food. He didn't look particularly worse for wear this morning, but of the three brothers, Rusty hadn't seemed to be consuming all that much alcohol. Which was probably why he'd gotten stuck with the food run.

"Your brothers feeling okay this morning?" I asked as he pulled the bags from the box.

"They will be once they get a few gallons of coffee and some breakfast in them." Rusty rolled his eyes. "I'm sorry about last night. Paul's a good guy, really. He's impulsive and wild, but he's not a bad guy."

"I assume you all are taking it easy today?" I asked, thinking he was more than a bit blinded when it came to his eldest brother. From what I'd seen, Paul was *not* a good guy.

"No, we're going hiking." He gathered up the bags and headed for the door. "Peter and Paul might be hungover as all get-out, but they're determined to get out there on the trail. It's probably going to start out rough, but hopefully the worst of their hangovers will be gone by noon. If we don't get back in time to put in tomorrow's food order, can you just duplicate what we got today?"

"Sure." I made a quick note by the register to remind myself. "And enjoy your day." I grimaced, glad I wasn't the one hungover and hiking a trail.

As soon as the morning rush was over, I took Elvis out for a quick pee-stroll around the office, then went back inside to tidy up the shelves and look over the remaining bags in the food box. When Mom came in at nine, I didn't argue about leaving. After updating her on the status of the camp store and our need to order more chocolate milk, I gathered up Elvis's leash and headed back to the house to change.

It was a gorgeous Saturday morning. Everything at the campground was running smoothly. Inspired by my guests, I was going to go for a hike—a long peaceful hike.

CHAPTER 9

*E*lvis lumbered onto his usual spot on the couch while I went back to my room to change into clothing more suitable for a long hike. I debated between shorts and pants, and ended up with the pants, thinking even with the exertion it would still be a little cool for shorts. Lately I'd been practically living in my sports bra, so all I needed to do was put on a wicking shirt, a light jacket, and grab my daypack.

Heading out into the living room, I put Elvis's collapsible bowl, two bottles of water, and an array of snack foods into the pack. I kept it semi-ready with a small first-aid kit, a rain slicker, a headlamp, and a packet of camp matches, and didn't think I'd need more than that plus the food and water. As I stuffed two more bottles of water and two Ziploc baggies with dog food into Elvis's doggie backpack, I noticed the hound watching me attentively.

"Wanna go for a hike?" I asked.

He was up and off the couch like a shot, belying that lazy bloodhound stereotype. Elvis could sleep, but when there was food or an interesting sniffing activity in the offering, he was suddenly full of energy.

I put his backpack on, making sure the weight was balanced and that the straps were snug but not uncomfortably tight. Then I grabbed the leash and clipped it on Elvis's collar before putting on and adjusting my own backpack.

We headed out, waving at the guests as we walked down the drive to cut through the RV area and take the Black Locust trailhead. I hadn't had more than an hour or two here and there to hike, and was excited to have an entire day to myself. Mom was right, I needed to take more me-time, and that was starting right now. Our guests had all arrived. The first day had gone without a hitch—well, *mostly* without a hitch. The morning rush had ended and all the guests were off enjoying their vacation. Mom was handling the store, and Austin would be arriving soon to take care of anything else. Plus I had my cell phone on me, just in case of an emergency. Not that I could quickly get back to the campground in case of an emergency.

I put that worrisome thought aside, determined to enjoy my day. I'd loved the Black Locust trail when I was a child. I'd seen my first black bear on this trail, and years later my first lynx. It was rocky, steep, and at the apex had an amazing view down on the lake. As a bonus, it veered off at the end to join up with the Red Fox trail that circled around to the north side of the lake. Equally steep and rocky, the two trails together were a tough eighteen miles out and back.

Not that I was going to attempt eighteen miles today. I hoped to finish the Black Locust Trail, then if I was feeling good, I'd do a bit of the Red Fox Trail. Coming back, I planned to take the Red Fox trail all the way to the campground and avoid traveling the more challenging Black Locust trail twice.

It would be a challenge either way. I hadn't attempted

either of these trails since I'd arrived. For one, I'd been too busy. Two, I wasn't sure I was up to that level of exertion at this point.

There was that little part of my mind that worried I might end up calling an Uber, like Tamara Boone had joked about this morning. Not that an Uber could make it out on either of these trails. Even if they had a four-wheeler, I doubt they'd get up the side of some of the boulder-strewn hills.

Were there Uber four-wheelers? Someone needed to make that happen.

Elvis and I stepped onto the trail and were quickly plunged into the shade of a canopy of scarlet oaks and red maples that I knew would be absolutely stunning in the fall. As we climbed, I passed patches of mountain laurel and little rocky alcoves. Elvis and I made several stops for me to catch my breath, sip water, and munch on the homemade parmesan crisps, the olives, and the assorted nuts and dried fruit that I'd packed. The trees had thinned out and sun was overhead when I turned onto the path to the overlook. There Elvis and I sat, ate our lunches, and enjoyed the view.

The lake glistened in the sun, gray in some spots, greenish in others, and blue toward the center. The rounded mountains came right to the edge of the water at the north side, while flatter marshy areas were toward the south. Across the lake I could see clusters of houses and small marinas. Motorboats crisscrossed the water with smaller fishing vessels hugging the shore. The breeze lifted my hair, drying the sweat on my back and ruffling Elvis's short fur.

We sat for almost an hour, just being in the moment. Then with a reluctant sigh, I rose.

"Come on, boy," I said to the bloodhound. "We've got time to do a few miles on the Red Fox trail, then we need to head back.

Elvis stood, stretched, then shook, ears and jowls flying.

With a laugh I wiped off some of the drool that draped across his face with my jacket sleeve, then we backtracked to the turn off for the other trail.

The Red Fox trail wasn't quite as rocky and steep as I'd remembered, and the easier terrain gave me a chance to really look at the foliage. Rhododendrons grew alongside the trail, far more massive than I'd ever seen in a domestic garden. I caught sight of a sweetshrub with its reddish-brown buds ready to burst open in the next week or two. I knelt down to smell the flowers, inhaling the citrusy-strawberry scent. After a few miles we turned around. Again, I walked slowly, admiring the dogwoods, the redbuds, and the sumac along the trail.

"Look Elvis." I paused to point out a tree. "It's a sassafras."

My namesake, and far more beautiful than me, in my opinion. I touched the deeply furrowed, thick, red bark, and admired the vibrant green, oval, mitten-shaped, and three-lobed leaves. I'd need to make sure I came back out earlier next spring in time to see the flowers, and in the fall when the leaves turned yellow with tinges of red.

Touching the bark once more, I kept walking down the trail, feeling as if the tree were a good omen.

I was distracted, thinking about the gorgeous variety of trees and flowering shrubs in the forest when Elvis almost yanked me off my feet, pulling me to the side of the trail.

I tightened my grip on the leash. "What do you smell, buddy?"

His nose was to the ground and he cast back and forth as he always did when he'd locked onto a scent. Elvis had spent most of our hike sniffing the ground, the bushes, the trees, and the rocks, but this was different. This was Elvis in focus-mode, when there was a scent-trail he felt absolutely compelled to follow. I picked up a jog, trying to keep up and wondering what on earth had him so excited.

With another yank that nearly pulled my arm from its socket, Elvis veered left onto a narrow side trail that was so choked with shrubs and weeds it was barely a deer track. I stumbled after him down the trail, glad I'd worn pants as the briars and twigs scraped at my legs.

It was always difficult to break a scent hound away from their genetic prime directive, but Elvis had an urgency to him this time that he usually didn't have when he was tracking down a rabbit or a fox. No, this was the sort of intensity my hound exhibited when we'd done our search and rescue classes. If he pulled the leash out of my hands and got away from me, I might not be able to call him back—not when he was fixated with this kind of intensity on a smell. And I was also concerned about what exactly he was tracking. Hopefully it wasn't something that would maul us and leave our half-eaten bodies behind.

I crashed through the bushes behind the hound, gripping the leash with both hands. The fact that something else had recently crashed through these same bushes took a few seconds to register. Broken branches, small plants that had been obviously stepped on. Whatever had been here before us had been big.

"Elvis, sit," I shouted as visions of a bear, or lion, or moose went through my head. Bear. We didn't have lion or moose here in Reckless, Virginia, so it was probably a black bear. I'd been reading up on them as well as the other local flora and fauna the last few weeks, so I knew they tended to run when they saw humans. Or lumber away, if not run. Still, this was their home I was hiking through, and I'd heard enough tales of mother bears defending cubs or the occasional attack, that I was beginning to panic.

Elvis was not panicked. He ignored my command, which wasn't all that unusual for a hound. They were purpose bred animals, independent and focused. When Elvis was on a scent trail, I swear his ears turned completely off. I was pretty sure a nuclear blast wouldn't deter him from a scent trail.

Bear spray. I probably need to start carrying bear spray when I'm hiking, I thought as I gripped the leash tight and tried to keep up with Elvis. Bear spray, and probably the vibration collar so I could get his attention if he pulled the leash away from me.

As we burst into a boulder-strewn clearing, I tripped over a rock, nearly face planting. When I got my feet back under me and looked up, I realized that Elvis had stopped and plopped his butt on the ground in the stance he took when he'd located whatever it was he was tracking.

Glancing over his shoulder and toward the overlook, I gasped. Then I fumbled for my phone and dialed 911, because it wasn't a bear Elvis was after, it was a body.

A dead body.

CHAPTER 10

$\mathcal{I}$ had to go back to the main trail to get a decent signal and tie a couple napkins around a tree branch to mark where the turn-off was for the side trail. I'd spent a few minutes convincing Shelly, the grumpy 911 operator, that I had indeed discovered a dead body—another one. Yes, I was the woman who'd discovered a dead body earlier this same month. No, I was not drunk or on drugs or prone to hallucinations.

After I felt reasonably certain that she believed me and that she was actually going to send help, I returned to the overlook, not wanting any hiker to stumble across the body, and also because I felt like it was important to safeguard the scene. Like my mother, I'd watched a lot of CSI and all of the Criminal Minds shows, and even though this might be a death by natural causes, I'd already been through one murder at my campground and was a bit paranoid.

Plus I recognized the dead man. It was Paul Mason.

I tied Elvis to a tree, then stood with my back to the body. But try as I might, I kept looking over to where he lay, unable to keep my eyes from something I definitely didn't want to see. He was sprawled on the rocks of the overlook, his head resting in a pool of blood. Next to him was his daypack, open with several items removed.

I forced myself to look away. *Thankfully the pack isn't where the blood is.* Shaking my head at the thought, I wondered why it had crept into my mind. Ruining a backpack didn't matter. A man was dead—that's what mattered.

My gaze slid back to the body of my guest, then over to the backpack. He'd stopped here for lunch. There was his water bottle, a crumpled-up paper bag and an apple core. On the ground next to the body were the remains of a sandwich and a thermos with its coffee spilled onto the ground and mixing with the pool of blood.

I edged closer, because the shock of finding a dead person seemed to not only make me weirdly concerned about them not getting blood on their backpack, but also made me curious as to what the deceased person ate for their last meal.

Grilled veggie with lettuce as the wrap holding the whole thing together. Only it was not held together, but spilled out on the ground. I envisioned Paul Mason collapsing, the food falling from his hand as he slumped over.

No, I didn't want to think about that, so I focused on the sandwich instead. It was quickly becoming one of the favorite options on the lunch menu. I often ordered one. They were so tasty with the spears of zucchini and carrots nestled together with onion, mushroom, and bamboo shoots. And I adored Sierra's spicy brown sauce, but I wasn't sure what the white powdery and chunky stuff was in the sauce. Sea salt? I'd never had anything like that in the wraps I'd eaten. I squinted at the food. It wasn't sea salt. It looked like the ground up pills I used to hide in Elvis's food back when he'd been on antibiotics.

"Sassy?"

I jumped what seemed like twenty feet when I heard Jake's voice behind me.

"What are you doing?" he asked.

I slapped a hand over my racing heart and turned to him, being careful not to step in the pool of blood, the spilled coffee, or the sandwich remains.

"Nothing. I was looking at the veggie wrap." I winced, realizing that I sounded like I'd gone off the deep end, scrutinizing spilled food next to a dead body. "I didn't touch anything. I was careful," I added.

"Okay." Jake gave me a puzzled look. "Why don't you wait over there by Elvis, where you don't have to look at this. I'll talk with you there as soon as I take a few pictures here. The sheriff and Sean are on their way.

I nodded and headed over to where I'd tied Elvis, standing beside him and stroking his ears. Our local sheriff and the deputy would be here soon. And so would the coroner. Watching Jake as he took his pictures, I wondered once more what had happened. Had Paul come here to have lunch, gotten dizzy, and hit his head on the rock as he'd fallen? Maybe someone had attacked him, hitting him on the head and killing him?

For a brief second I panicked that there was a murderer in the area who had stalked and bludgeoned Paul Mason to death off of a seldom-used side trail. Then all my experience watching CSI shows kicked in and I realized there wasn't a spray of red like I would expect if someone had hit Paul. And it looked like the injury was to the part of his head against the rock. The wound would be faceup if someone hit him, wouldn't it?

Maybe he'd died of natural causes and hit his head as he slumped over. It seemed like a lot of blood, but what did I know? Yes, natural causes. That was a much less alarming thought than a killer-stalker. In my mind I pictured Paul walking down the overgrown side trail He would have sat undisturbed on the overlook rocks, enjoyed the gorgeous view of the valley below while eating his lunch. Then he'd died. Peacefully. With absolutely zero foul play involved.

Please let that be the case, I pleaded.

Jake approached me, pulling his notepad and pen from his pocket. "Stef just texted that she's on the main trail with Oliver and Sean. While I'm waiting for them, why don't you go ahead and tell me what happened."

I peered around Jake at the body, then quickly looked away. "I know him. He's one of my guests. I know him."

"I'm so sorry, Sassy." He put a hand on my shoulder and squeezed. "Do you need to sit? A drink of water?"

I pulled the bottle from my backpack and took a drink, sinking down to sit beside Elvis. Jake squatted in front of me, blocking my view of the body. I was pretty sure that was intentional, and I appreciated his concern.

"It's Paul Mason," I said, feeling a bit better.

"Paul Mason?" Jake frowned. "The guy who registered a complaint about Sierra last year? The one you were debating whether or not to cancel his reservation?"

I nodded. "I feel terrible because he was a bothersome guest and I was counting down the days until he and his brothers were gone. And then I find him dead..."

"Sassy, you didn't wish the guy dead," Jake reminded me.

"I know, I know." I took another sip of my water and snuggled Elvis closer. "He was driving fast on the entrance road when he and his brothers arrived and acted like an entitled jerk. Then I found him arguing...with someone."

For some reason I didn't want Jake to know that it was Sierra I'd seen arguing with Paul. I didn't think she'd done anything to harm the man, but I also didn't want Jake to think badly of her. Paul had complained to the police about Sierra threatening him, and a year later I caught her doing the same thing. Sierra might have a good reason for her intense dislike of Paul Mason, and I didn't want her to get a bad reputation with the police over whatever was going on between them.

Had been going on. I shut my eyes, trying to get the image of the dead man from my memory.

"Last night Paul was drunk and half-naked dancing around the fire with blue paint on his chest and a beer box on his head," I continued. "He told me that the night before he'd peed on someone's tent, probably because he was drunk and couldn't find the restroom."

"Are you sure you didn't kill him?" Jake teased. "Because I doubt there's a jury in this county that would convict you if you did."

I laughed, only slightly appalled at his dark and somewhat inappropriate humor. "No, I didn't kill him. Did he...was it hitting his head that caused his death? Doesn't seem like he would have fallen hard enough for it to have killed him, but there's so much blood..."

"Sometimes if you fall and hit your head on a rock in the wrong place, you can die," Jake said. "Or even break your neck. Or maybe he had a medical condition. We'll have to wait for Steff to weigh in on that."

"A medical condition?" I frowned wondering what the local coroner would find. "Paul was in his early thirties. And he looked fit—outside of all the drinking, that is. Was it the drinking? He was hungover but okay this morning—at least that's what his brother Rusty said. Do people spontaneously die of hangovers?"

"No, but people do die of dehydration because they were hungover and went on a rigorous hike." Jake looked around. "Do you know if he hiked out alone?"

I thought for a second. "Rusty said they were all going hiking today, but I didn't actually see any of them leave.

Their cabin looked unoccupied when Elvis and I went by around ten o'clock, but maybe they decided to stay in and nap, and Paul went out on his own? I really don't know."

"So tell me what happened—but start with this morning," Jake said as he scribbled something in his notepad.

I told him about Rusty picking up the food items, and that the man had apologized for his elder brother's behavior. "He looked tired, as if he was a little hungover as well," I added. "He said they were going to eat breakfast, then head out for a hike. I think they expected to be out all day since he asked me to duplicate their food order if they weren't back before seven."

Jae nodded. "They order food every day?"

"Every day so far. Breakfast and lunch. The last two nights they've cooked dinner on the grill in front of their cabin but they always order breakfast and lunch, and some-times buy snack items at the store. Paul got roast beef and Swiss with horseradish. Peter got turkey and hummus on whole wheat. And Rusty got the grilled veggie wrap with lettuce as the wrap and extra sauce." My voice hitched as I remembered something. "He said Paul sometimes ate his sandwich because he really liked the veggie wraps. That's what he was eating. The veggie wrap on lettuce. His brother's sandwich was his last meal."

Jake patted me once more on the shoulder. "You remember everyone's food orders? I'm impressed."

I gave him a watery laugh in response. "No. I just remem-bered because Rusty made a point of telling me. Evidently they order the exact same thing every day."

"It's still impressive," Jake said before getting his pen and notepad ready once more. "So what happened after they picked up their food?"

"I didn't see them again after that. I headed out around ten this morning with Elvis for a hike. Mom said she and

Austin could handle things, and I needed a break," I told Jake. "I took the Black Locust trail that goes up to the lake overlook, then I was feeling good so I veered off on the Red Fox trail for a few miles, then turned around to head back to the campground."

"That's a solid hike." Jake smiled reassuringly. "Some nice views off the Black Locust trail this time of year too."

I nodded, then told him about Elvis's insistence on taking the little side trail to this site. "I don't think the path is well traveled. I mean it's clearly a trail, but it's really overgrown with brambles and brush. The overlook is amazing though. I'm surprised more people don't come this way."

I was rambling, thinking again about the body and the blood pooled on the rocks.

"Elvis took you down this path?" Jake gave the hound a puzzled look. "Is he a retired police dog? Does he have SAR training?"

"He's a rescue so I'm not positive, but I believe his original owner used him for tracking game," I explained. "We did a few years of search and rescue training together after I adopted him, but he's never been trained as a cadaver dog, and I didn't send him out on a search, so I really don't know what made him find this man."

I was glad he had. Otherwise who knew how long Paul Mason would have been lying here in the woods. I imagined his brothers would have eventually sent up an alarm, but no one would have noticed him missing before then.

And where *were* his brothers? Had they stayed back at the cabin, or gone on the hike with him? If so, then why was Paul dead in the woods, with the other two nowhere nearby? Had they left him here and hiked on? Or had he turned back on his own, paused for lunch and to enjoy the view, then died?

"Was there anything else you remember seeing?" Jake asked. "Anything notable on the trail? Did you touch the body at all? Roll him over to see if he was okay, or check his pack?"

I shook my head. Other than my fascination with his sandwich and the fact that his pack had escaped getting blood on it, I hadn't seen anything that caught my attention —anything besides Paul Mason's body, that was.

The sandwich. I opened my mouth to tell Jake about the weird white bits in the sauce, then shut it. Paul had most likely suffered a massive heart attack, or an aneurism, or had fallen and hit his head in the wrong place and died. There was no crime. Whatever it was, Paul had probably added it to the sandwich himself.

Steff, our local EMT and coroner, the Sheriff, Oliver Norman, and Deputy Sean Cork came out of the path into the clearing. Another man followed Steph, with a stretcher under one arm, and a huge bag slung over his other shoulder. Jake got up, telling me he'd be right back, and went over to the others. They walked to the body, then watched Steff and her assistant as the two went to work.

Half an hour later, they all conferred, Steph waving her hands around and speaking in soft tones. The sheriff turned to Sean and Jake, and talked to them for a minute. Then both men walked away, Jake coming toward me and Sean headed down the trail.

"They've got some local volunteers blocking the path," Jake said. "And an ATV to help move the body once they get it down the trail."

"Do you need anything else from me?" I asked, wanting nothing more than to get back to the campground at this point.

"I'd like to walk back with you, if that's okay," he said. "Even with Elvis by your side, I'd feel better if someone went with you. Plus, I need to notify Paul Mason's next of kin, ask them some questions, and go through Paul's belongings. I was hoping you'd point out their cabin. I'm assuming you'll want to speak to them as well."

"I probably should, although I'm not sure what to say beyond giving them my condolences." I grimaced, thinking that the other two Mason brothers might consider any condolences from me to be insincere. But I didn't want Paul dead. There was a big difference between being annoyed at a guest for drunken rowdy behavior and wanting them dead.

"It was natural causes, wasn't it?" I asked Jake as we slowly made our way down the path. "Or maybe he was hungover, fell, and hit his head?"

"Right now we're calling it a suspicious death."

I stopped abruptly and turned to face Jake. "Suspicious how? Was he murdered? Did someone hit him on the head and arrange the body to make it look like a fall?"

Jake held up a hand to stop me. "Stef says there are signs pointing toward a drug overdose, but we didn't see any paraphernalia nearby or in his pack. He might have taken pills instead of snorting or injecting, though."

"Drugs?" I gasped.

Paul Mason had certainly liked his booze, but *drugs*? I'd naïvely assumed no one at the campground would be taking illegal substances. Pot I could imagine. It was legal in Virginia, and I should probably expect to get a whiff of someone's joint eventually, but hard-core drugs?

"Drugs," Jake repeated. "From what Stef said, it might be an accidental drug overdose, or she could be wrong and it he might have died from a preexisting medical condition. Even if Paul *was* taking something, that might not have been what killed him, but we still need to check."

I thought back on what Jake had said earlier. "You'd mentioned dehydration. I know there have been dehydration deaths with distance runners or backpackers, but could someone out on a day hike be dehydrated enough to die?"

Jake shrugged. "Dehydrated, got dizzy, fell and hit his head? I can see that happening. Or it might be a bunch of things all together. Drugs. Dehydration from the hangover and the exertion. Maybe he passed out and whacked his head on a sharp rock. But we won't know until Stef does her thing and issues the report. Until then, the sheriff is calling it a suspicious death. Sean is looking into the man's medical history, and the rest of his background. I'm supposed to talk to the family and gather as much information as I can."

"So not a murder?" I asked, hoping that was actually true. "A drunk, hungover man over exerted himself hiking and had a heart attack, or got dizzy, fell, and died from the head wound? Or he was on drugs and accidentally overdosed?"

"Any of those things are possible. Nothing's off the table right now." Jake started walking again and I hurried to keep up. "We need to know if Paul Mason was taking any medications, either legally or not, and if he had any health conditions. That's where I'm going to start."

"Is there a chance someone slipped him the drugs?" I asked, thinking again about the white stuff on the sandwich as well as the spilled coffee.

Jake came to an abrupt stop. "Why? Do you know someone who wanted him dead?"

Sierra. No, she'd just been angry. She couldn't actually kill someone, could she?

Everyone could kill someone, given the right motivation. Self-defense. Protecting a family member. But Sierra was my friend and I just couldn't imagine her as a murderer.

"Paul did pee on a camper's tent," I reminded him, realizing that was a silly reason to murder someone. "Except I don't know whose tent it was. No one complained, so I'm guessing the guy might not have known what happened. Maybe he thought a coyote peed on his tent or didn't even notice."

Jake's lip twitched at one corner. "Okay. Other than the peed-tent guy, who else might have an issue with Paul Mason?"

I caught my breath, once more thinking of Sierra and the argument behind the camp store. Should I tell Jake about that? Should I tell him about the white powdery stuff on the sandwich? They'd collected the food in one of those evidence bags, so if there was something on the sandwich that killed Paul, they'd soon know it for sure. And I just couldn't rat out my friend.

"I mean, there is Sierra Sanchez-Blue," Jake commented casually. "They had a run-in last year that was serious enough that Paul Mason complained to the police. She supposedly threatened him. If we're making a list of potential suspects, we'd be negligent not to have her on it."

He was right, but that didn't mean I had to like it. Sierra was *not* a murderer.

Sierra was delivering the orders this week instead of Flora. She'd had a confrontation Thursday with Paul. And now he was dead.

But surely other people might have hated Paul as well.

"A few of the campers have complained about the noise, and Paul's drunkenness at the bonfire," I said. "I don't think anyone was angry enough that they'd resort to murder, but there might have been something going on that I wasn't aware of."

Jake sighed and kept walking. "So we're back to accident, accidental overdose, or previous medical condition then. I'd like to talk to your guests though, if you don't mind. Just some informal questions to be thorough, and you're welcome to be there with me. With your guests leaving next week, it will be easier to question people while they're here than having to track them down when they're back home and at work during the day."

I slumped, hating the thought that my guests were going to be questioned by our sometimes-deputy about another guest's death. I understood. Jake had a job to do, and I'd do everything I could to help him. But now the whole campground would know that Paul Mason had died and that the police were calling it suspicious. Even if it ended up being ruled natural causes or an accident, they'd wonder if this was a safe place to stay. They'd think twice about returning to a campground where someone had *died* the week of their stay. I could see the reviews now. *Had an amazing vacation, except for the murder and police investigation, that is.*

I was a horrible person for worrying about reviews on Camper-Go or Yelp when a man had died this morning.

"Mom has the list of guests and their locations at the camp store," I told him. "I do want to come with you so I can introduce you and vouch for your official capacity as well as explain what happened and reassure my guests that they're safe here. After we speak to Paul's brothers and you check his belongings, we'll work our way through the campground. I just want to warn you that it might take more than one day. Lots of them went out fishing early this morning, or for hikes. They might not be back until late this evening."

Jake nodded. "That's not a problem. Just keep track of anyone who checks out early so I can follow up with them later. I'll try not to disturb your activities. I know you've got something planned for this evening. Dried flower wreath-making, wasn't it?"

I smiled and shook my head. "The bottle-cap art was last night. Tonight we're having a campground potluck with a cooking contest. Prizes for the winner. You're welcome to join us."

"I really don't want to bother you," he said. "This is police business, and I'm already inconveniencing you and your guests. I'm not going to add eating your food to my list of transgressions."

I laughed at that. "Eating my food is the least of those transgressions. Seriously, Jake. Mom made a giant batch of her famous mac and cheese. There's no way we're going to eat it all. It's not like I can give the leftovers to Elvis either. His stomach doesn't do well with dairy. Or pretty much any food besides fish, sweet potatoes, rice, and venison."

Jake reached a hand down to scratch the bloodhound's back. "Venison, huh? That's good to know. I'll make sure to save Elvis something this fall, if I manage to bag a buck."

"Save *me* something too," I teased. "Ground venison. Deer bologna. Send it all my way."

"I'll remember that," he promised. "Even if I only get one deer, I've always got too much for me alone."

"I'll take all of your extra." I smiled at the thought of a freezer full of venison. Then my smile faded as we came out of the woods and into the campground right by the Masons' cabin.

CHAPTER 11

$\mathcal{R}$usty Mason answered at my knock. He was still in his hiking clothes with his muddy boots placed by the door.

"Is Peter here?" I asked him. "This is Deputy Jake Bailey. We need to speak to both of you."

Rusty turned slightly, calling into the one room cabin for his brother before looking back at Jake, then at me. "What did Paul do this time? Was he arrested? Do we need to go down and make bail?"

His defeated tone told me he wouldn't have been surprised if that were the case. I wondered how many times he and Peter had needed to bail their brother out.

"No, your brother hasn't been arrested," Jake replied. "Can we come in?"

Rusty stood aside and we both entered the cabin. It was surprisingly neat given that three men were sharing the small space. A cot with an air mattress had been pushed against one wall, and duffle bags were lined up against the other wall. Hiking gear, fishing poles, and several cases of beer were wedged between the bed and the dresser. There had been a giant cooler on the front porch that I was sure was full of more beer. I wouldn't have been surprised if their truck didn't have another cooler full of ice and beer as well, but maybe not. That much beer seemed excessive for a week-long vacation, but given what I'd seen them consume just last night, I might be underestimating the Mason brothers' tolerance for alcohol.

"I'm sorry to tell you that your brother's body was found off the Red Fox trail this afternoon," Jake said, his voice and expression somber.

Rusty's eyes widened and he took a step back. Peter looked equally stunned, and somewhat confused.

"No! You can't be serious. Is this a joke or something? What happened?" Peter asked.

"We're not sure what happened yet," Jake told him. "He was found at a rocky overlook off a side trail. We don't know a cause of death yet."

"I can't...I can't believe this." Peter's face scrunched up and he turned away. "No. Just...no."

"I'm so sorry for your loss," I said, feeling like the words were inadequate. They'd just lost their brother, a young man who they'd probably been expecting to see come through the door any moment. It was clear from their expressions that this was a horrible shock. Whatever paranoia I'd had about murder earlier, these two clearly hadn't wanted their brother dead.

"Given his age and the unexpectedness of your brother's demise, the sheriff's office is investigating the incident," Jake said as he pulled his trusty pen and notepad from his pocket.

"Investigating?" Peter spun around, his face pale. "Incident? I thought he'd slipped and fallen off the overlook or something. You think he was murdered?"

"He appears to have collapsed at the overlook," Jake told him. "We don't know what happened or why he might have collapsed. And while we don't currently suspect foul play, we need to gather all the information we can while our coroner is conducting her end of the investigation."

"She's doing an autopsy? I don't think Paul would have wanted that." Peter wrung his hands together. "I can't believe he's dead. I can't believe he's in some morgue right now. This has to be a horrible joke."

"I'm so sorry, Mr. Mason, but it's not a joke." Jake's voice was firm, but kind.

"We need to know what happened," Rusty told his brother. "None of us likes the idea of an autopsy, but it's the only way we'll get results. If he died of a heart attack, or a stroke, or something, then I want to know."

Peter drew in a deep breath, then let it out with a shaky sigh. "Okay. I want to know what happened. I just...this all feels so unreal."

"I'm sure it does. Your brother was a young, fit man. Which is why I'm hoping you'll let me ask you both a few questions." Jake gestured toward the cot and the chair. "Would you rather sit?"

Peter collapsed in the chair as if his legs were yanked out from under him while Rusty went to stand next to his brother.

Jake readied his pen. "Had your brother been ill at all? Complaining of chest pain, headaches, breathlessness, or nausea?"

Peter and Rusty slowly shook their heads.

"He was fit," Peter said. "Healthy. I mean, he took some pills for cholesterol or blood pressure or something, but it was minor. He was physically active. There was no warning that this sort of thing was going to happen. No warning at all."

Jake made a few notes, while I wondered that someone supposedly so fit and healthy was taking pills for cholesterol or blood pressure in his early thirties. That didn't sound very healthy to me.

"Tell me about this morning," Jake asked when he was done writing.

"We were hungover," Peter admitted. "Rusty went to the camp store to get our food. We made coffee, ate, then left to go on our hike. Figured we'd sweat it out, you know? We hit the trail around eight or eight thirty. We planned on taking the Red Fox trail out to where the Sumac trail joins in, follow that one for five or so miles, then turn back."

Twenty miles. Hungover. I winced at the thought.

"How much did your brother drink?" Jake asked. "Both last night and on average in a regular week?"

Rusty shrugged. "Last night? Probably twelve beers and four or five shots of Fireball."

I was pretty sure my eyes bugged out at that.

"We're on vacation," Peter explained. "Paul usually has a beer or two in the evening, but unless he's going out or playing poker with the guys, that's it."

I glanced over at Jake's notepad, pretty sure he was writing *possible alcoholic* down on it.

"What did he have to eat and drink?" Jake continued. "This morning, I mean."

"Egg and ham on croissant." Peter glanced at me. "We order breakfast and lunch through the camp store. Last year we used to go to that coffee place in town to get food, but it's really convenient having it delivered here. We don't usually bother to cook anything besides dinners."

"He also had coffee," Rusty added. "The decaf I picked up when I got our food order. We were rushing to get out on the trail, so he poured most of the pot into a thermos to take with him. Paul likes his coffee, even if he had to switch to decaf a few years ago."

No doubt because of the same heart issue that caused him to take either cholesterol or blood pressure medicines, I thought. It was looking more and more like the guy's heart had just given out on him.

"He left our hike early," Rusty added. "None of us were doing all that good the first few miles, but Paul started having some stomach issues and turned back only an hour or so in. We teased him about being hungover and not holding his liquor, but I figured he must have eaten something that didn't agree with him."

"It didn't seem serious," Peter chimed in. "Rusty and I kept hiking and Paul turned back. When we returned and he wasn't here, we figured he got a second wind and went fishing or something."

"Instead he was lying out in the woods. Dead." Rusty shuddered and lowered his head to his hands.

"Was he married? Is there a girlfriend or someone else we should contact?" Jake asked.

That got Rusty's head up with a jerk. He shot a quick glance at his brother before looking away.

"He and his wife divorced a couple of years back," Peter said in measured tones. "There's no one else to notify. We're his closest family."

"Beyond the cholesterol or blood pressure issues, did you know of any medical conditions he might have had? Any other medication he was taking?" Jake waited for both men to shake their heads. "Did you see him take anything regularly? Aspirin? Antacids? Anything like that?"

Both men shook their heads once more.

"Can you let me know who his doctor was so we can check on any medical information you two might be unaware of?" Jake asked.

Rusty snuck another look at his brother. This time his expression showed fear along with grief. Peter continued to look directly at Jake, not even giving his brother a glance.

What was going on here? I was no detective, but clearly there was something between these men that they didn't want Jake to know about. Had there been a fight out there in the woods? Had one of them hit Paul over the head with something, then let him walk back to the cabin alone, thinking he'd be okay? And now they were worried they'd be on the hook for at the least manslaughter?

Or was my imagination running into overtime? All those CSI shows had me already envisioning their guilt when they might just react differently to grief than I expected. They were both probably in shock, and had reason to be. I'd been shocked as well to find Paul Mason dead off the trail.

"I don't know who his doctor is," Peter said. "I guess he had one, but he never mentioned who it was."

"Can I check his bag for anything?" Jake asked. "Just to be thorough?"

Peter shrugged. "Sure. It's over here."

"There might be a doctor's name on his pill bottle," Rusty spoke up. "He kept the meds in the glove box of the truck. I can go get them if you want."

Jake nodded. I followed Rusty out, telling Jake I'd be in the camp store when he was done. I was starting to feel like an interloper in both this investigation and in these men's grief. It was awkward, just standing around while Jake went through a dead man's belongings and asked his family questions about his medical history. Yes, the man was dead, but I wasn't sure I'd be so willing to talk about someone's private medical concerns with anyone who didn't need to know that information lurking around.

Rusty glanced back at me as we went down the porch steps. "I can't believe he's gone. He was fine this morning. A little headache from the booze, but fine. When we were out on the trail he started having stomach cramps and intestinal stuff. Not to be gross or anything, but he wanted to come back where he could be near a bathroom."

Rusty headed over to the truck as he spoke, and I followed, not wanting to be rude and walk off while he was talking to me.

"I figured maybe he'd eaten something that didn't agree with him." Rusty shook his head. "I wonder if that was a sign or something. Maybe if we would have turned back with him, we could have done something or called someone and he would be alive right now. Instead he died alone."

I blinked back tears, not sure what to say to comfort this man. "It was a beautiful overlook. He'd stopped to have lunch, so he must not have felt that bad, or maybe after he headed back he started feeling better?"

Rusty turned to face me. "You found him? Were you hiking to the overlook and saw him, or did you hear him call out for help? What happened?"

"I was hiking, and my dog took me down a small side trail to the overlook," I explained. "He was already gone when I found him. It looked like he was eating lunch and collapsed, but I really don't know."

Rusty clenched his jaw and looked away. "I let him have my sandwich. I wasn't all that hungry after breakfast, and Paul said he'd forgotten to pack his roast beef, so I'd given him my grilled veggie wrap. He loves those things, even though he likes them with the flour wrap instead of lettuce. I hope he enjoyed it before he died. I hope he had a nice lunch with a beautiful view. He loves this place, you know. He loves hiking here."

And I'd been about ready to ban all three of them from the campground. This would have been Paul's last trip here even if he'd lived, and that made me feel a bit guilty.

"The hiking here is very nice," I awkwardly replied. "I

don't know how long it takes for the coroner to do her investigation, but hopefully you'll soon have answers."

"I hope so. I just wish we'd turned back with him. I hope…I hope it was just a heart attack and not something we did that killed him." Rusty opened the truck door and opened the glove box, pulling papers and a pair of pliers out and putting them on the passenger seat.

"You mean drinking?" I asked softly. "Or something else? Maybe you all had a fight, like brothers do? And punches were thrown?"

Rusty gripped a prescription bottle and stood up straight to face me. "Paul and Peter had an argument last night and it got a little physical. It wasn't bad—nothing that hasn't happened before. I'm sure Peter's just sick about it. I mean, what if one of his punches did something to Paul, and he died from it?"

I wasn't a medical professional, but I couldn't think of any punch that might kill someone ten hours later.

"Did he fall and hit his head during the fight?" I asked. "Did Peter choke him or something?"

"No!" Rusty's eyes widened. "It was just stomach punches. We don't fight like that. Just stomach hits and sometimes in the shoulder."

"What were they arguing over?" I asked, thinking that two drunk men could probably argue over just about anything in the world.

Rusty sighed. "Hope."

I blinked, not expecting such a philosophical answer.

"That's Peter's wife," Rusty explained. "Soon to be ex-wife. They split up soon after Paul and Miranda divorced. Paul slept with Hope, but it was after she and Peter separated, so Paul figured it was okay. Peter didn't. But they worked it out. Blood is thicker than bootie, you know?"

"Uhhh." I honestly didn't know what to say about this soap opera of a family.

"I'm sure Peter feels horrible. He and Paul were okay come morning, but that fight is weighing on him, I know. Here." Rusty shoved the pill bottle into my hand. "I need to take a walk and think a bit. Tell the cop I'm down by the dock if he needs me."

I watched Rusty walk off, then looked down at the prescription bottle. Warfarin. 5mg once a day.

Blood thinner. Not cholesterol or blood pressure medicine, but blood thinner pills. Well, that would explain the excessive bleeding from the head wound. Maybe that also explained Paul Mason's death. He'd been drinking, which even I knew wasn't a good idea while on heart medications. He was hungover, no doubt dehydrated, and most likely had the runs according to Rusty. He got dizzy after stopping to each lunch, fell over, hit his head, and died.

Maybe this *was* just an accident after all.

CHAPTER 12

J took the bottle in to Jake, let him know where Rusty was, then left him talking to Peter and going through Paul's belongings. Unhooking Elvis from the railing of the cabin porch, I slowly walked down the gravel path.

The campground was idyllic this afternoon—like the death of a guest hadn't been significant enough to register even a blip on Mother Nature's radar. The spring sun was warm on my skin as I made my way to the camp store, Elvis by my side. Insects buzzed, reminding me that in a month or so I'd be cursing them and covering myself with bug spray each morning. The air was crisp in spite of the sunshine. The smell of the lake and the verdant chartreuse of the leaves and grass filled my nose with every inhalation. It was beautiful. It was just as beautiful as I'd remembered from those vacations when I was a child. This was my paradise, and no matter how much work it took to run the campground and make it profitable, I still loved it here.

But someone had died. It was the second death we'd had in less than a month, and that weighed on me. Daryl's demise had been due to greed and theft, but Paul? Was it a medical condition that had finally ended his life? Or something else?

I took Elvis into the office with me, leading him behind the checkout counter and looping his leash on a hook. Mom came out of the backroom, smiling when she saw me.

"How was your hike?"

"Great, except for finding a body," I replied, moving Elvis's doggie bed a little to the side so he could still snooze, but we wouldn't be tripping over it.

"What? A body?" Mom stared at me, open-mouthed.

"A body." I filled her in on what had happened, letting her know that I'd probably be busy the rest of the day escorting Jake around to question the guests.

"I'd been hoping Paul Mason and his brothers would decide to cut their vacation short and leave, but him dying didn't figure into any of that," Mom came over to give me a quick hug. "I'm so sorry you found him, honey. Don't worry about this affecting the campground. I'm sure other places have had a guest die while hiking and it didn't cause them to go out of business."

Now that I'd been thinking about it, Paul Mason's drunken antics had probably annoyed guests more than his passing or having to answer a few questions from our local sometimes-deputy.

"I'm hoping the coroner determines Paul's death to be accidental or due to an underlying medical condition," I said to Mom. "Evidently he was on blood thinners."

"Drinking that much on blood thinners?" Mom grimaced. "Why are they even investigating this?"

"The coroner had some concerns about a possible drug overdose, so they're being proactive, just in case," I explained. "Everyone leaves on Thursday, and the sheriff felt it best to interview people while they were still here. Until the autopsy results are in, cause of death is determined, and the police get the details of his medical conditions from his doctor, Paul's death is going to be investigated as suspicious."

Mom clucked her tongue in sympathy. "How did his brothers take the news? They must be devastated."

"They were. He was young and his death was so unexpected. Rusty was worried that Peter would feel guilty because the two of them had fought the night before. Something to do with Paul sleeping with Peter's estranged wife. Rusty said they both threw some punches, but all was forgiven by morning. Still…"

"Paul slept with his brother's estranged wife?" Mom shook her head, eyes wide. "What an idiot. He must have known that would eventually come out and that it would affect his relationship with his brother. Maybe I'm old-fashioned, but in-laws are off-limits, even when they're soon-to-be-ex in-laws."

"I got the impression nothing was off-limits to Paul Mason." I agreed with Mom, but knew that others didn't feel the same way. And from the short time I'd known the man, what Paul Mason wanted, Paul Mason got. Or at least tried to get.

"I don't want to do the sheriff's job for him," Mom commented. "But if Paul was on blood thinners and got into a fist fight, he probably had a whole lot of excess bruising. He might have even had internal bleeding that contributed to his death. Peter might be feeling guilty because he *is* guilty."

I hadn't thought of that. "His brothers mentioned he turned back on their hike because he was having stomach problems. Rusty indicated he was having…um…a gastric emergency? An urgent urge to go number two? His brothers thought maybe he'd eaten something that didn't agree with him."

"That could have been the case. Or maybe his digestive issues were because he'd been bleeding internally from the fight last night," Mom pointed out. "Also, after all that drinking, dehydration could have made him wobbly and a head wound could be fatal for someone on blood thinners."

I frowned. "There was a lot of blood," I said, remembering the pool of red. And the coffee. And the sandwich.

"Then my money's on internal bleeding. That or someone poisoned him."

Mom's tone was joking, but I blinked in surprised. "Really? I mean, the coroner did mention a possible overdose, but I assumed that meant Paul was taking illegal narcotics or was prescribed something and accidentally took too much, not arsenic or something."

"I wonder what sort of easily accessible drug could have a fatal interaction with blood thinners," Mom mused. "Maybe Peter Mason was angrier about Paul and his estranged wife than Rusty realized."

"I really don't know," I replied, appalled at the suggestion, and thinking that Mom really had been watching too many of those crime shows.

"Stuff with vitamin K counteracts blood thinners," Mom said, surprising me with this weird knowledge. "So spinach or kale or something like that?"

"Death by kale? Seriously? Plus, wouldn't that take a lot of spinach and kale?" I wondered. "I mean, I can't imagine that a leaf of spinach on a sandwich would kill a guy."

"No, you're probably right and it was just natural causes," Mom agreed. "Alcohol also thins the blood, from what I've read."

"What exactly *have* you been reading, Mom?" Had she enrolled as a pre-med student at some point and I hadn't realized it? Did she spend evenings reading online medical journals while I'd been stuck with books on tulip mania and hummingbird migration patterns? Maybe I should change up my reading habits, because as far as I knew no one ever died from tulips or hummingbirds, and death was starting to be disturbingly frequent here at my campground.

Mom waved a hand. "Oh, you know me. Always wanting to learn something new and different. Between those crime shows I love to watch and the classes at the community college, I've picked up a few things."

"Well, I hope Paul died from a pre-existing medical condition," I said. "A heart problem plus his drinking plus the dehydration are probably enough for a natural-cause of death. All this investigating is just a precaution."

That gnawing feeling in my stomach told me that this was all wishful thinking on my part.

Mom went back to the house to take a break and I restocked and cleaned up a bit in the camp store. I'd just made a fresh urn of coffee when Jake came through the door. The sometimes-deputy looked exhausted. He ran a hand through his hair, sighing as he lowered himself onto a stool by the counter.

"Coffee?" I gestured toward the urn. "It'll be ready in five minutes."

He looked at his watch.

"Mom's taking a break and won't be back before the coffee's ready," I said. "And you look like you could use a cup."

"I could," he agreed. "Black please, with one sugar."

I pulled a go-cup and a lid from the rack, dumping a packet of sugar into it before grabbing a cup and lid for myself. I could use a cup of coffee as well. It had been a long morning. And afternoon.

"Weird as it sounds, I won't be sad if I've spent all day running around interviewing people and bagging stuff out of the Masons' cabin only to find out the guy had a heart attack from some sort of congenital defect," Jake commented, running his hand through his hair once more.

"Finding out he overdosed on narcotics would be horrible," I agreed. Horrible for him *and* horrible for his family.

"His brothers insist alcohol was the only drug Paul ever indulged in. No drugs, no tobacco, not even caffeine in the last few years. Which means if it's drugs, Paul might not have knowingly ingested them."

"Murder," I said, that gnawing in the pit of my stomach returning at the thought.

"One murder in Reckless this year is one murder too many. Two…well, that's not the small town I thought I knew and loved," Jake said with a grimace.

"Even if it's murder, that doesn't necessarily reflect on the town or its residents," I reminded him. "And it might not have even been premeditated murder. Mom and I were speculating about some kind of over-the-counter drug interaction with his blood thinners."

Jake blinked at me, then laughed. "All right then, Sherlock. You and Watson have it all figured out."

His tone was teasing and friendly, so I didn't take offense. "What, you didn't realize my mother has a medical degree, a law degree, and a PhD in forensic science?"

"Does she really?" Jake shook his head and chuckled. "I mean, I kinda believe it. Your mother is one smart cookie."

I smiled, warmed by the comment. "She *is* smart. But we were just throwing ideas around. I'm sure the poor man had a heart attack. In the next day or two Stef will announce his death was due to natural causes, and we'll all go on about our lives."

"Or not." Jake's face hardened, and suddenly he looked all-cop. "Steff and the sheriff will go through the contents of the man's pockets and day pack. I've got his medicines, and I bagged his toothbrush and other toiletries. I also took the coffee grounds, the cup he drank from this morning, and the remains of his breakfast as well as the leftovers of what he'd eaten before they'd set out on their hike. How the heck a guy feeling hungover and sick ate a breakfast sandwich and a cold hamburger is beyond me."

"Greasy food sometimes settles a hungover stomach," I told Jake remembering my college days. "And I don't think they ate much last night. Paul was probably starving this morning."

With an empty stomach gnawing from excessive alcohol consumption. Poor guy. But bagging all the leftover food, wrappers, coffee grounds, and cup from the cabin seemed a bit overkill for a just-in-case investigation.

"You found something suspicious," I accused Jake, guessing that he probably wouldn't tell me much about an active investigation.

But it seemed that small-town policing and a retired park police/sometimes-deputy didn't have the same rules as the detectives I'd read about in my mystery books.

"Just covering all my bases," Jake said. Then he lowered his voice. "Peter seems nervous, as if he blames himself for his brother's death. I don't want to miss anything only to find out that Paul Mason was murdered and the evidence was conveniently disposed of."

I nodded. "Although Peter might be feeling guilty because he and his brother had a fight the night before. It's got to be difficult to lose a family member, when there were bad feelings between the two of you the evening before his death."

Jake stared at me. "You witnessed this fight?"

"No, Rusty did." I told him about what the youngest Mason brother had revealed to me when getting his brother's medication from the car's glove box. "I'm sure the alcohol didn't help things, but Peter was really angry."

Jake snorted. "You think? Your brother sleeps with your wife—separated or not, she's still your wife. I'd have punched him too."

I shivered a little at his tone—partially because Jake was scary like this, and partially because he was really attractive like this. Weird. I'd never been the sort to go for the alpha-male, but Jake wasn't like the guys from those billionaire romances I'd devoured all last year. He was strong, confident, stable. He was like that immovable object, that rock you knew no amount of TNT could crack. But at the same time he was kind, funny, and the perfect...neighbor.

Yeah. The perfect neighbor. And friend. Because that's all I wanted at this point in my life.

"I get him being mad, but the three of them were close, and Peter's wife was on her way out," I said. "I can't see him killing Paul over this. If the fight contributed to Paul's death, then I'm sure it was accidental."

"If the fight contributed to Paul's death, then a court of law will determine if it was accidental or not," Jake replied. "Things like how much bruising there was, how violent the fight became, and if Peter knew his brother was vulnerable because of his blood thinner will weigh into whether he'll be charged or not. Of course, we're just throwing ideas out. Nobody knows anything concrete right now."

CHAPTER 13

The coffee maker made a gurgling noise and I turned to pour the steaming liquid into our cups. I was putting the lids on when the door opened and Mom came in.

"Jake. It's wonderful to see you." Mom sighed. "Well, it would be wonderful to see you under other circumstances. I'm sorry you're working on such a lovely afternoon."

"Me too, Mrs. Letouroux. I'd rather be fishing," he said.

I turned back and handed him his coffee. "I'm taking Jake around to talk to the guests," I told Mom. "I've also got the roster so he can make notes about who is camping where."

I thought it might be a good idea to check off people as we spoke to them as well. With so many guests, it would be easy to miss one or two.

"I'd love a copy of that roster if you can get me one," Jake said. "Names, addresses, phone numbers and other contact information would be helpful, as well as when they arrived and where they're camped."

Normally I would never give out a guest's private information, but this was official police business and I wasn't going to insist Jake go get a warrant. The man had enough to do today without having to write up an affidavit and track down a judge to sign off on it.

"I'll print out a copy when we're done," I told him.

"I'll do it." Mom shooed us toward the door. "You both get going. I'll take care of things here."

Jake held the door for me and I preceded him out, waiting on the porch for him. We walked in silence side-by-side down the drive to the RV sites.

"I thought we'd start here first," I told him. "I'm not sure who is in right now and who isn't, so we'll mark off the people we talk to on the roster, and you can come back to the others later."

"I've got some business cards we can leave for people who aren't around," Jake said. "They can call me and I'll swing by. It'll save time if I don't have to run around trying to track people down for the next few days."

"Tonight is the camp-cooking potluck," I reminded him. "Most of the campers planned to be here for it."

He shook his head. "I wouldn't feel right disturbing people in the middle of their dinner, especially when we're not sure the guy just didn't have a heart attack. Besides, I've got horses to feed and tools to clean up. I was doing some barn repairs when the call came in and I left everything laying all over."

"Well, you're welcome to come by when you finish your chores. Or tomorrow. Whenever is convenient," I added awkwardly.

We started at the far end of the RV sites with a woman about my age who'd arrived in a pop-up camper. Shelane White had been towing what looked like a small, flat trailer behind a Subaru Outback when Mom and I had checked her in, so I was surprised and impressed to see the pop-up in all its expanded glory.

The camper was decorated with strings of lights in the shape of daisies. A huge red and tan sisal rug was spread at the bottom of the camper steps. Shelane had put a tent canopy in front of the entrance, overtop of the rug. It provided a sheltered spot for a pair of tall, bright green rubber boots, a pair of director's chairs, and a low table. On the table sat a caddy with silverware, a basket full of plates, bowls and cups, and a silver bucket holding a bouquet of daisies that matched her lights. The owner was over by the grill, fileting fish on a paper-covered picnic table.

"Looks like you had good luck today," I said as she waved me over.

"Not a bad morning." She grinned. "Although any morning on the lake with a fishing pole in my hand is a good morning. I've got enough here to make fish stew for tonight's potluck."

"Mmmm," I said appreciatively. Then I gestured toward Jake and made the introductions.

"I'd shake your hand, but I don't think you'd appreciate that right now." Shelane laughed and held up two very fishy hands. "What can I do for you today, deputy?"

"Paul Mason, one of the other campers here, was found deceased just off one of the trails late this morning." Jake held out a reassuring hand at Shelane's gasp. "We're not sure what exactly happened, but just to be proactive we're talking with the other campers to see if there was anything they may have seen or noticed."

Shelane frowned. "Paul Mason. Which one was he? The backpacking guy with the long hair? Or was he that old guy with the little teardrop camper?"

"He and his two brothers were staying in one of the cabins. He was around thirty." I winced. "The guy with the blue paint, dancing around the bonfire last night?"

Shelane's eyebrows shot up. "The drunk guy! What

happened to him? Did he stumble off a cliff? You said he was found out on a trail? Lordy, that man was so drunk I couldn't imagine him being able to get out of bed this morning, let alone go hiking."

"We're not sure what happened yet," Jake interjected. "Do you remember anything about him?"

Shelane paused a few seconds, staring off into the distance before slowly shaking her head. "I don't recall seeing him other than at the bonfire last night, but I'm not sure I'd recognize him without the blue paint. I pass the cabins early in the morning when I'm heading out to fish, but there aren't a lot of people up then. It's pretty quiet—which is what I like."

"Did you overhear anyone talking about him?" Jake asked. "Or anyone arguing?"

She shook her head again. "I try to stay out of any drama. I'm here to relax and fish, not get caught up in other people's nonsense. As for arguing, the only people I've heard fighting is that couple with the little girl." She inclined her head toward the big RV parked a few spots down. "I can't remember their names. Annie and Chip or something? The little girl is Lexi. Cute as a button. I feel sorry for her. The dad's always yelling and the woman crying."

I caught my breath, wondering if what I'd assumed was just marital tension had escalated into domestic violence. A death might not be the only problem needing a law enforcement intervention in my campground this week.

Jake slanted his gaze over toward the fifth-wheel camper. I did as well and noted no activity in or around the spot.

"I don't think it's anything physical," Shelane hurriedly added. "It's not like the fighting was enough for me to be worried about the woman or the child's safety or to complain. I just think they're going through some relationship troubles, and this vacation isn't helping. From what I overheard, the guy thinks his wife is cheating or is going to cheat or something. He was accusing her of eyeing someone and flirting. She says it's not true." Shelane shook her head and gave me a rueful smile. "I just told you I don't like drama, but here I am gossiping about my campground neighbors. I shouldn't have said anything."

"No, I appreciate you saying something," I told her. "I'll keep an eye out for Lexi and Adelaide."

I also would find the opportunity to speak to both the woman and her daughter without Charlie, just in case they needed help. It might just be typical marital strife, but I knew that sometimes people needed a lifeline, needed to know someone noticed, that someone cared enough to offer help. If Adelaide or Lexi were feeling scared, trapped, and in danger, I wanted them to know they had options—and that they had people on their side.

Jake and I thanked Shelane for her help, then continued on. By the time we'd spoken to every available guest, I was exhausted and I could tell Jake was as well. No one had seen anything or heard anything. Most of the guests didn't even know who Paul Mason was until I mentioned the blue paint and drunken dancing at the bonfire. I'd half expected one of the tent campers to complain that someone had peed on his tent, but none of them spoke up about the urinary incident, confirming that they hadn't noticed or had believed it was an animal. There went the peed-on-my-tent motive. I was returning to my belief that he'd died of natural causes.

Until we got to cabin seven, that was.

I'd purposely tried to leave the cabins around the one the Mason brothers occupied vacant, hoping to avoid any complaints with a buffer zone between their cabin and the others. But we'd had a few last-minute guests, so I'd reluctantly put Denver Twigg in cabin seven which was right next to the one the Masons were staying in.

Denver Twigg was a large man in every sense of the word. The man had ducked to clear the top of the threshold at the entrance to the camp store, and had barely made it through the opening without needing to turn sideways. He was a balding man in his late forties. What remained of his straight brown hair was tied back in a low ponytail, and he seemed to favor baggy jeans, loud Hawaiian shirts, and white Converse sneakers. I'll admit I'd taken one look at the man and wondered why he was asking to rent a cabin for the week, since he didn't meet my stereotypical vision of an outdoorsy-guy. His dimpled smile and soft-spoken voice only added to my confusion.

Then I'd seen him unload boxes of art supplies, an easel, and several large canvases from his car.

Denver sat on the porch of his cabin on a stool, his easel and canvas in front of him, a table with paints and scattered supplies at his side. He was intent on his work, glancing over at us with surprise when we were less than a few feet from him.

"Oh! Hello! Miss Sassy, isn't it? Are you here about the potluck tonight? I'm afraid I didn't have time to make anything, so I won't be joining in."

"The campground events are never mandatory," I said with a smile. "But you're welcome to put out some chips or snacks as your offering. Not everyone is cooking something."

"I might just do that." He motioned toward the cabin. "I brought enough Doritos for an army."

I smiled. "I'll gladly come by for Doritos. Denver, this is Jake Bailey. He's a retired officer who is a part-time deputy here in Grant County. Jake, this is Denver Twigg of Arlington, Virginia."

The man set down his paintbrush and reached out to shake Jake's hand. "Hope this isn't an official visit, Deputy

Bailey. Is possession of six bags of Doritos against a Grant County law?"

Jake laughed. "Not that I'm aware of. But sadly, I *am* here on official business. A guest at the campground was found deceased off one of the trails this afternoon, and although his death might have been due to natural causes, we're asking around, just in case."

"Of course. I'm happy to help any way I can, but I have to tell you that I really haven't socialized much with any of the guests. I'm here for inspiration, and to paint when creativity strikes."

I glanced at the painting as Denver and Jake spoke. It was an abstract rendition of the woods, the lake, a fishing pier, and dogwood trees. I recognized all the elements from the campground, and although it wasn't my style, I definitely liked it. The colors and shapes were energizing and something about it all definitely felt like spring.

"They weren't that bad Thursday night, but Friday night I came close to complaining." Denver's words broke through my reverie at his painting. "I don't mind the music and the loud conversation, even though I'd hoped for a more quiet week here. That fight worried me though. I seriously thought someone was going to end up needing an ambulance."

"I'm so sorry," I told him. "Let me comp you a night of your stay to make up for the disturbance."

He shook his head. "It wasn't your fault. People are people, and you just gotta deal with their quirks, you know? Honestly, now I feel kinda bad for being annoyed since the man is dead. Was it the one with the wife, or the one who slept with her who you found off the trail?"

I winced, bothered that the fight had been loud enough that he'd actually been able to make out what the argument was about.

"Can you tell me more about the fight?" Jake asked, scribbling in his notebook. "It was over one of the men's wives?"

I shot him a quick glance because I'd already told him what Rusty had said. I guess this was how detective investigations worked, though. You asked questions as if you didn't know anything at all and saw where the story led you.

"I don't know how it started or when it exactly turned into a fight," Denver told him. "They came back early from the bonfire, carrying boxes of beer and complaining about Miss Sassy telling them to leave. They went inside, then the young one with the auburn hair came out and got some bottles of hard liquor out of their truck. They were playing classic rock—Aerosmith and Rolling Stones and stuff—but it wasn't too loud so I ignored it. I could hear them talking, laughing, and shouting. Then suddenly there was more shouting then laughing and talking. One was yelling at the other for sleeping with his wife or ex-wife. The other was calling the ex-wife names and saying she had initiated the whole thing and that he was better off without her. Next thing I know there were some crashing noises and thumps, like the fight had turned physical. I went to the door and saw they'd taken it outside, which was probably a good thing. Three grown men in a cabin that size? They'd have torn the place apart fighting in there."

I glanced over at the cabin in question, mentally going through my visit there earlier. Nothing had seemed damaged, although it would have been hard to tell with all the stuff they'd piled inside. This was something I should mentally prepare for, though. Not all guests would be considerate of the campground property, and I needed to remember that's what the security deposit was for.

"They were rolling around on the grass and onto the gravel of the drive," Denver continued. "Punching each other, mostly in the gut, and wrestling—scrabbling with their feet trying to get on top. The younger one, that red-haired guy, was yelling at them to stop, trying to pull them apart. The fight didn't take too long. I think they were drunk and they got worn out, because after a few minutes, they just lay there, breathing heavy. Then the older one of them got up, staggered over to the bushes and puked. They all went back inside and things were quiet after that."

Jake scribbled for a bit then looked up. "What were your thoughts about that fight? Was there a clear winner? Lingering bad feelings afterward?"

Denver shrugged. "It was kinda a train wreck, you know? I couldn't look away. They were both drunk and I didn't think either was doing any serious damage to the other in that condition. I think they were just working off steam, getting something out that had been festering for a while. And once it was out in the open, the anger kinda went away. Although maybe they were just close to passing out from booze and adrenaline."

I exchanged a quick glance with Jake, back to believing this whole thing had just been a perfect storm of a heart condition, hangover, and over exertion. Peter Mason might feel guilty about that fight last night, but from Denver's first-hand account, it didn't sound like it was the sort of altercation that would lead to internal bleeding serious enough to kill someone ten hours later.

"And you said the argument was over the one guy sleeping with the other's wife? Or ex-wife?" Jake confirmed.

Denver nodded. "I've never been married or anything, but I can imagine how it would hurt if a best friend or a family member betrayed me like that. Blood is supposed to be thicker than water, you know? Family and friendship come first. Anyone that does that, that betrays my trust like that, isn't truly my friend. And if they were my brother or sister? Well, I don't know if our relationship would ever be the same. We'd be family, but there'd always be that hurt, that knowledge that I didn't matter enough for them to keep it in their pants, so to speak. There's forgiveness, but sometimes even forgiveness doesn't repair a rift like that."

"But there didn't seem to be any lingering bad feelings when they all staggered back inside?" Jake asked.

Denver laughed. "There didn't seem to be any feelings beyond the desire to pass out in the bed and sleep it off. Like I said, they all went back inside, and I didn't hear anything else for the rest of the night. I saw the youngest one up early and heading to the camp store. He came back, right after. About twenty minutes or so later, they all went out for a hike. I was here all day, doing sketches, and reading a book on native Virginia plants that was on the bedside table with a couple of other books when I arrived. I was outside painting around two or three and saw two of the guys come back from their hike. They've been pretty quiet all afternoon, but I would expect that given the amount of booze they drank last night. I assumed they were trying to sleep the rest of their hangover off."

Jake closed his notepad and stuck it back in his pocket before pulling out a card and handing it to Denver. "Thank you, Mr. Twigg. If you remember anything else, please don't hesitate to call me."

Denver held the card between two paint-stained fingers. "It's a darned shame that man died so young like that. He and his brothers were drunk and rowdy, but you don't really know someone from just a few days on vacation, so I try not to judge. I hope you find out soon why he died so his family can grieve."

CHAPTER 14

I got back to the camp store and saw Austin putting the cleaning supplies into the back room. It was after five o'clock and escorting Jake around on his interviews had put me behind on tonight's activities.

"Here." I picked up an armful of signs that were in the corner of the store room and shoved them into Austin's hands. "Go to each of the campers and if they're participating in the potluck, give them a sign to post in front of their campsite. And hurry. This whole thing is supposed to start in half an hour and we're not ready."

"Okay." Austin took the signs. "Anything else I can do, Miss Sassy?"

"Come back to the camp store when you're done with the signs," I told him. "But that's the priority for now."

He saluted me and took off out the door. I dashed into the main part of the store, grabbing the tickets from behind the counter.

"Do I have time to go get the mac and cheese from the house?" Mom asked as she watched me running around like a chicken with my head cut off.

"Yes. I'll be here for a while," I told her. Plus I intended on putting the "be back soon" sign on the door when the potluck started. My phone number was posted for emergencies, and hopefully the guests would recognize Mom and me by this point if they needed to find us.

While Mom headed over for her mac and cheese, I set up a table by the firepit, lugging a decanter of sweet tea, a bucket of ice, and some cups out as well. That done, I set up a box and the tickets for people to vote for their favorite potluck item. The red signs were numbered, and I realized as I put the tickets out that I'd forgotten to ask Austin to note down which sign he'd put in front of which campsite. Drat. Now I'd need to run around and do that myself so I could quickly determine who the winner was and get them their prize. For a second I thought about asking Austin to head back out when he was done to do it, but then I realized it would be a good excuse to not only socialize with the guests, but to sample the potluck offerings myself.

I'd just finished getting everything set up when a familiar van pulled up beside the camp store. I waved as Sierra got out. Glancing at my watch, I frowned. She always picked the orders up at seven, and it wasn't quite five thirty yet. If we had any late orders, I guess I'd just need to text them over to her.

I took one look at her expression as she climbed the porch, and I knew something bad had happened.

"What's wrong," I asked once we were inside. "Is Flora okay? Deshaun?"

"They're fine." She leaned against the counter and clasped her hands tightly together. "Sassy, I heard what happened. It's all over town that you found Paul Mason dead in the woods. People are already looking at me funny, as if they think I had something to do with it."

"Why would they think that?" I asked, as though I hadn't

been worried about this very thing. "I found him in the woods, off the trail. You weren't...you weren't out there hiking this morning, were you?"

"No, but I don't have a verifiable alibi for my whereabouts this morning or afternoon," she confessed. "I was roasting beans while my new employee, Mary Alice, watched the coffee shop. It's getting too much for me and Flora to do on our own, so I finally hired someone. And when Flora goes to college, I'll need the help anyway."

"But the police don't even know if Paul died from natural causes or not," I told her. "Even the town gossips can't seriously believe you had anything to do with his death just because you were alone roasting beans when he died."

Her eyebrows gathered together. "But people know about last year. I threatened him. In public. Right on Main Street with people watching. I told him he needed to leave Reckless and never come back, or I'd kill him."

"Oh, Sierra." I went to her and put my arm around her shoulders. "He had a heart condition. He was on blood thinners. The coroner will determine that he died of natural causes, and all the gossip will die down. Just hang in there."

Sierra shook her head. "Robert said that Noranne told him that Dani from the sheriff's office said that Stef's preliminary coroner's report says foul play."

It took me a second to follow that chain of rumors. I wanted to be outraged, to reassure my friend, but I'd just spent most of the afternoon walking around with Jake so he could interview the guests "just in case." He'd bagged up leftovers from the trash and coffee grounds "just in case." That was a lot of "just in case" for a guy who'd died of natural causes. He'd said Stef was concerned about a possible drug overdose. Paul's brothers had insisted there had been no drug use. But there had been that white stuff on the sandwich at the crime scene.

No. Not crime scene. I couldn't think like that right now, even though my mind had been going in that direction ever since Elvis had led me to Paul Mason's body.

"And just how were you supposed to have killed him?" I asked, giving Sierra's shoulder a squeeze. "Sneak over in the middle of the day, follow him and his brothers down the trail without anyone seeing you, then wait for him to turn back—which you psychically knew he'd do—and follow him to the overlook before whacking him in the head? Or stuffing pills or something down his throat?"

She laughed, but it ended on a bit of a sob. "Rumor is I put something in his food delivery. The order sheets have everyone's name on them so I can label the bags. People think I poisoned his breakfast sandwich or something."

I wanted to counter that, but honestly it *was* a pretty good murder method. Well, except for the fact that Sierra would have to be stupid to poison Paul Mason after having several public altercations with him—*and* stupid to kill him via food that came from her coffee shop, and was prepared by her.

Sierra wasn't a stupid woman. But she wasn't very cautious when it came to her emotions surrounding whatever was between her and Paul Mason.

"It's just rumors," I told her. "A bunch of small-town gossip. I'm sure the final report will reverse the 'foul play' thing and say he died of natural causes. Then everyone will go back to talking about Celeste Crenshaw's pig or something."

Sierra sniffed and looked over at me. "I want to tell you what happened. No one knows—no one but my family and Paul Mason, and his brothers. But I want you to know why I'm so furious at him, why I hate him so much, why the police are going to come to me as a suspect if it turns out he was killed."

I eyed her. "You don't have to tell me if you don't want to.

I'm here for you. You're my friend and I'm happy to listen and do all I can to support you, but I don't want you to feel like you have to reveal things to me that you want to keep secret. It won't hurt our friendship any if you keep private things private and don't share them."

"I want to tell you." She took a deep breath and slowly let it out. "Last summer, when Len owned the campground, we were only making coffee deliveries. Len put our menus out and we offered a limited delivery service on food. It wasn't as efficient or as popular as what you're doing, but once or twice a week one of the campers would call and ask us to bring out a bunch of sandwiches or a dozen muffins or something."

I nodded, waiting patiently as she paused a few seconds before continuing.

"Flora helps at the coffee shop, but I want her to focus on her school work and have time to be a kid. I worked from the day I could get a job washing dishes at a local diner for pay-under the table. We…we didn't have a lot of money growing up and if I wanted something besides jeans from Goodwill and a hand-me-down coat with a tear in the sleeve, I needed to save for it myself. It wasn't just clothes. If I wanted to go to the Friday game and buy something at McDonald's after, then I needed cash for that. Although when you're a teenager clothes are important. Kids are mean, you know?"

"I know." I patted Sierra's shoulder in sympathy while she got back to what happened last year.

"I wanted Flora to have a different childhood, so all she did was help in the coffee shop on weekends, and make the occasional delivery run. She was hanging out here at the campground a lot, and I didn't really mind. Len was a good guy, and I trusted him. He was so sweet to Flora, letting her take a kayak out on the lake if she wanted. She could swim, sunbathe, hang out at the bonfires. I was seeing less and less of her, and it worried me, but I tried to let it go. Teens are learning to be adults, to live their life outside of constant adult supervision. Deshaun and I talked, and we both decided that as long as her grades were good and there were no signs of alcohol use or drug use, we'd let Flora have a lot of freedom."

I had a bad feeling about where this was going. Had Paul Mason gotten Flora drunk? Had he...did he...? But surely Sierra would have reported it to the police and had him brought up on charges if that had been the case.

"Flora came home one night tipsy and upset. She was sixteen and we thought she'd been out with friends, had a few drinks, and either had a disagreement with one of her gal-pals or was rejected by a boy she liked. It wasn't until the next morning before she told us what really happened."

"Paul Mason didn't...he didn't...." I couldn't even get the words out.

Sierra shook her head. "I don't know where Flora got the alcohol and she wouldn't tell me, but she did say she ended up partying with the Mason brothers first at the bonfire then back at their cabin. I was angry at Len Trout for not noticing and stepping in, but he probably hadn't known. Then Flora told me Paul got...handsy at their cabin, and things were going in a bad direction—a real bad direction. The youngest brother, who I hate to tell you isn't much older than Flora, pulled Paul off of her. He helped her get her clothes back situated, drove her around until she'd calmed down, then brought her home. As much as I wanted to see Paul Mason dead, I owe his youngest brother. If it hadn't been for him, the whole night would have ended badly."

"It already ended badly." I started pacing. "Too bad Paul Mason is dead, because I'd like to kill him myself."

Sierra's lips twitched. "You'd need to get in line behind Deshaun and I. The only reason people are eyeing me about his death is because unlike my husband, I can't control my temper."

"But why didn't you go to the police?" I knew the answer as soon as I'd voiced the question.

"Flora begged us not to. It's a small town and I didn't want her to have to go through all the scrutiny of pressing charges. I didn't want her having to go into school every day with people whispering about her, wondering whether she was just a tease or had lied for attention, or people speculating on what she was wearing at the time and blaming her for drinking."

I winced, knowing she was right. Society was not kind to women who were victims of sexual assault. All criticism turned their way while the sympathy for "careers and lives ruined" went to the accused. It wasn't fair, and I hated that Sierra and her family had made a difficult choice to keep quiet about it, all to protect their daughter.

"Sierra, I'm so sorry." I gave her a quick hug, knowing now why she'd been the one picking up the orders and making the deliveries this week. It hadn't had anything to do with Flora's homework or AP classes, and everything to do with her protecting her daughter from possibly seeing her attacker every day.

"Thanks." She hugged me back. "I wish I'd never confronted him. I wish he'd just gone home this coming Thursday and I'd never seen him again. I wish he hadn't died. Well, in all honesty I've wished a lot that he was dead, but I didn't want it to happen at your campground or after I'd publicly said I was going to kill him."

I couldn't help but chuckle at that. "Technically he didn't die at my campground but in the state park. So the State of Virginia should be the one bearing the guilt on Paul Mason's death."

Sierra swiped a finger under one eye. "I appreciate you having my back, Sass."

Sass. I kinda liked that even shorter version of my nickname.

"I hope you're right," she continued. "I hope he just died of a heart attack or liver failure from all the drinking. I hope in few days both you and I can go back to our lives, and that your campground doesn't suffer any blowback from this whole thing."

I sighed, stepping back. "The other guests seem to be okay. Jake has been very discreet about his questioning. He's told all the campers that this is just a formality since everyone will be leaving next week, and he's implied that Paul was just another one of those tragic deaths that occur when someone who's hungover, and has a medical condition tries to push themselves on a trail."

"People die in national parks and on state park trails all the time," Sierra agreed. "Lots of them are suicides, but lots of them are also accidents or people getting in over their head in the wilderness. It's sad. Not that Paul Mason's death is sad—I'm gonna put my opinion out there right now. He hurt my daughter, and no one does that and lives. While I'm glad that karma got him, I really don't want to take the blame for his death."

"I completely understand." I snapped a picture of the list with the food orders, then handed it to Sierra, remembering something I'd wanted to ask. "Hey, is there any chance you can share your sauce recipe from the grilled veggie wraps?"

She grinned and shook her head. "Nope. It's an old family secret."

Figures.

"You haven't changed it in the last day or so have you?" I asked. "Tweaked it? Added a spice or a thickening agent or something?"

Maybe the white stuff had been lumps of cornstarch? Although I couldn't imagine Sierra not noticing that, as meticulous as she was about the food she made.

"It's the exact same recipe that we've had for three generations. I wouldn't dare change it. I make a batch up twice a week and keep it at the shop for orders, although I've been thinking about bottling it and selling it," she added.

"I'd absolutely buy some." I glanced at the list in her hand. "Do you mind adding a grilled veggie wrap on there for me? Using lettuce as the wrap? With extra sauce?"

It was the exact same thing Rusty had ordered, the sandwich Paul had been eating when he died.

"Sure, no problem." She grabbed a pen from the counter and added my order to the list.

I saw movement outside the camp store window and realized that Austin was returning with his arms empty of signs, and that a few campers were beginning to wander around with plates and cups in hand.

"Stay for our potluck," I encouraged Sierra. "Mom's made her famous mac and cheese."

She shook her head and smiled. "It wouldn't feel right given everything that's happened. Plus I didn't bring anything for the potluck and that's not fair. And it would be horrible if I ran into the other Mason brothers."

She was right. I gave her another quick hug, and walked her toward the door.

"Wait, you said the youngest brother, Rusty, isn't much older than Flora?" I frowned. "His registration said he was twenty-two. I have a copy of his ID in case of emergency."

Sierra sighed. "I don't know for sure, but he told Flora last year he had a fake ID so he could drink and that he was eighteen at the time. I wasn't about to out the guy who'd saved my daughter from being raped, but he's not twenty-two."

I scowled, remembering how I'd thought Rusty had looked young, but had doubted my judgement at the time of their check-in. At fifty-eight, everyone under the age of thirty seemed like a kid to me. My radar was seriously defective, and I didn't trust myself to guess anyone's age under fifty at this point. I was going to need to take another look at Rusty Mason's ID. I wasn't about to go policing everyone's camper, cabin, or tent, but drinking in the common areas wasn't going to be allowed if the guy was truly under twenty-one.

But underage drinking wasn't the worst problem I was facing right now. A guest had died. And it hadn't yet been determined whether he'd died from natural causes or foul play. Plus a friend was hurting and scared that she'd be blamed for the death.

I put my arm around Sierra's shoulders again and gave her a quick hug. "It'll all be okay. I'm sure we're worrying over nothing, and that he drunkenly took too much medicine, or took something that interacted with his meds, or that he had a fatal heart condition he'd been hiding from his family. It'll all be okay," I reassured her.

And I was determined to make sure it would be okay, even if I had to turn into a Sherlock Holmes and investigate this myself.

CHAPTER 15

*S*ierra left and I finished setting up. Mom returned with her mac and cheese in one hand and Elvis on his leash in the other. The dog wagged his tail to see me, then turned his attention back to the large dish of food I was taking from my mother.

"Oh no you don't," I told the hound. "No mac and cheese for you. But I do have a nice peanut butter filled bone to occupy you so everyone else can eat undisturbed."

Mom got the serving utensils for the mac and cheese, while I got Elvis's bone. Then I sent her off with a plate and utensils so she could take the first round of potluck sampling. Mom had been cooped up in the camp store all day, and I knew she wanted to get out and walk a bit.

As people came to our table, I dished out the mac and cheese, sneaking a bit for myself. I also sold sweet tea and drinks from the cooler I'd stocked from the backroom fridge. Everyone seemed to be having a wonderful time, and the box with the votes for best potluck food was rapidly filling up.

We were running it on the honor system, assuming that everyone who was eating was also offering something or another of their own. The best food would probably run out before the potluck was over, but that would happen whether a few non-participating campers grabbed some food or not. I hated for anyone to miss out because they hadn't brought any food to share. And I made sure everyone knew that all potluck contributions were welcome, even if that was a few bags of Doritos or a box of Twinkies.

"I brought you back a plate," Mom called out as she came around the corner. "The couple in cabin four has grilled bratwurst, and the family with the vintage Shasta camper in spot five has this amazing guacamole. Oh, and I made sure to grab you some of the fish stew from Shelane, the woman with the pop-up camper. I had to practically wrestle someone for it. That fish was going fast. I got some for myself and I think it's getting my vote for best potluck."

"I think your mac and cheese is getting my vote," I told her. "I've been sneaking bites as people were coming to get their samples. You've outdone yourself, Mom. This is your best batch yet."

She beamed, pink rising up her neck at the compliment. "Thank you, honey. But you might change your mind when you taste this fish stew."

She handed me the plate and I stepped to the side, letting her serve two families who'd come up for mac and cheese. I'd just taken a bite of the fish stew when I saw Jake pull into a spot next to the camp store. With my plate in hand, I went over to his truck and waited for him to get out.

"Here to finish up the interviews?" I asked him.

"Yep. The horses are fed and set for the night, so I thought I'd come down and hopefully be able to talk to those people who weren't in earlier this afternoon."

"Everyone's walking around sampling food," I told him. "It might take you a while to find who you're looking for. If you're missing anyone, you can always swing back in the morning. Except for the hard-core fishing crowd, most people usually sleep in until eight. And I don't have anyone checking out until Thursday this week, so you've got time."

"Thanks. I might swing by in the morning. I don't want to interrupt your potluck event," he said.

"A man died. You're not interrupting anything." I looked down at the plate, scooting my food around with my fork. I wanted to find out if Sierra was a suspect, if she was really in trouble.

But instead I kept my mouth shut and ate the fish stew. Mom was right. It was good. But it was nowhere near as good as her mac and cheese in my opinion.

"Let me know if I can help," I said after I'd swallowed the bite. "I'll either be at the camp store, or in my house. And if I'm not there, Mom will know how to reach me."

Or he could always just text me. Duh. The guy had my phone number, after all.

"Hi, Miss Sassy!" A high-pitched voice called out. I looked over to see Mom dishing a spoonful of mac and cheese onto a plate held tight in the little hands of Lexi.

"Hi there, Lexi." I walked over to her. "What do you like the best at the potluck so far?"

"The brownies." She shot her mom a sideways look. "I liked the Doritos the painting-man had, but Mom says that's not really potluck food."

"Any food is potluck food," I told her. "And if you want to vote for the man giving out Doritos, you go right ahead."

I handed her a ticket. She set her plate of food to the side and I watched as she scrawled something nearly illegible on it before sticking it in the box.

"I like Doritos, but I liked the brownies better," she announced.

I made a mental note to be sure to tabulate her vote to the guest who'd provided the brownies, no matter how unreadable the scribble was on the ticket. Picking up her plate of food, she skipped off to where a few other kids were seated at a picnic table.

"I'll take just a small spoonful of the mac and cheese," Adelaide told Mom as she held her own plate out. "Honestly I'm full, but I heard a few of the campers raving about it, so I need to have at least a bite."

"You can always save it for tomorrow," Mom told her as she scooped some onto the woman's plate.

I watched, working up the nerve to ask Adelaide some difficult questions.

"Do you mind if I talk to you for a quick moment? Just over here where you can still watch Lexi," I added as Adelaide glanced over at her daughter.

"Sure." She followed me away from the table and to a quiet spot by the fire pit.

"I need to ask if everything is okay with you and Lexi," I started out. "A few people have mentioned some loud arguments between you and Charlie and have expressed concern about your safety." I held up a hand at her red-faced protest. "I want to help. If you need a safe place to stay, resources to help you get away and get on your feet again, I can help with that. You have options, and I'm happy to help you work through them."

"It's not...he would never..." She held her plate in one hand and brushed her hair back with the other. "I'm so embarrassed. We're just going through a rough patch, but Charlie would never hurt me or Lexi."

Her voice wavered so I motioned for her to sit.

"There's more to abuse than physical violence." I kept my voice soft, trying to tread carefully here. "You love him, and I know you don't want to think someone you love might hurt you, but it happens. Other guests are concerned. *I'm* concerned. I had my worries that first day when you all checked in. There's no reason to be embarrassed about any of this. We all need help sometimes. Please, let me help."

She scooted the mac and cheese around with her fork, then swiped a hand over her eyes. "I'd hoped this vacation would right things between us, but it's worse. He's worse. The accusations, the anger…"

I felt my own eyes tearing up. "Oh, Adelaide. I'm so sorry."

"I am too." She sighed then looked up, her eyes meeting mine. "He thinks I'm cheating on him. Back home I blamed his moodiness on grief over his mother's death and stress over my starting to work outside the home. Then he started accusing me of not being committed to our marriage or Lexi, saying the distance between us was my fault. After we get here, he tells me that he knows I've been cheating on him. I swear I've never cheated on him. Never!"

I frowned. "Was there a male friend of yours he's been jealous of? A co-worker? One of the dads at Lexi's school who might be newly divorced? I wonder why after all these years of marriage, he suddenly thinks you're cheating?"

Adelaide shrugged. "I don't know. I went back to work this year when Lexi started school, so maybe that's where he came up with this crazy idea? I do have some male co-workers, but I don't see any of them outside of work. And my friends are married. I get together with some other moms for playdates, but the only time I see their husbands is if Charlie and I are going out to dinner with them as couples."

I shook my head, equally perplexed. There had to be something that had given Charlie these ideas.

Or maybe not. Some people were paranoid and jealous and got caught up in their fears. Having Lexi in school and his wife back to work might have been what started Charlie down a path of imagining that his marriage was in trouble and his wife was straying. Either way, it wasn't healthy for

Adelaide and Lexi to live in an environment of anger and distrust.

"Maybe it would be best for you both to temporarily have some distance between you? Is there someone you and Lexi can stay with for a few months while you both attend couples therapy?" I asked her.

She gave a watery laugh. "Charlie would never go to a therapist. Never. But you're right. Once we go home, I think Lexi and I might move in with my sister for a little while. Although I hate to do that. It feels like I'm giving up on my marriage. I love him. I want the man I married back."

I kept silent, feeling terrible for the woman and wishing that some miracle would occur and everything would be alright. When my marriage had fallen apart, I'd said pretty much the same thing. I'd still loved Richard. I'd wanted the man I married back, wanted him to love me like he used to do. But he'd found another woman and wanted a divorce. I couldn't rewind time. I couldn't change the present. All I could do was walk forward into the future and create a life without him in it.

I'd survived. I'd survived something even worse than my divorce. But that wasn't what Adelaide needed to hear right now while she was confused over her husband's accusations and trying to figure out how to fix her marriage.

"I'm glad you have a sister you can turn to," I told her. "Hopefully you have other family and friends to help you as well, but if you need me, I'm here. My mom as well. If things get too stressful in the RV, I can always put you and Lexi up elsewhere."

She smiled. "Thank you, but I really can't afford that."

"No charge," I said. "In fact, why don't you come back to the office with me. I'll get you a key, and go put some linens on the bed. That way if you want to go there, even in the middle of the night, you can."

I had a cabin free right now, and didn't have a reservation for it until next week. It wouldn't be a big deal to have Lexi and Adelaide stay in it. All it would cost me is some extra cleaning and laundry. And I got the feeling it would do the woman good to know she had an out, had an option to being cooped up in an RV with Charlie if things got tense.

"Are you sure?" she asked. "I wouldn't want to put you out or anything."

"It's no bother at all." I stood and waited for Adelaide to do the same. "Besides, the cabin is right across from the man with all the Doritos.

She laughed. "Well then, I'll definitely take you up on your offer. Lexi will be thrilled to be next to Dorito Man."

I got Adelaide the keys, then ran over to put sheets on the bed and make sure the cabin was guest-ready. When I returned to the camp store, Mom's mac and cheese was almost gone.

Everyone was having fun at the potluck, dropping their votes for "best food" into the box by the camp store. I loved seeing my guests cheerful, enjoying their vacation, and getting to know each other. Hopefully they were making new friends—ones they'd keep in touch with after they went home. Hopefully they'd be back next year.

Mom came up beside me to take over manning the voting box. "Go. Get more food before it's all gone. Make sure you stop by number twelve at the tent sites. They made the best campfire dump cake I've ever had. Although, to be honest, I've actually never had a campfire dump cake. It's good, though."

"Then that's where I'm heading." I took a paper plate and some silverware and started over to where the tent camping area was. Walking around the back of the house to get to the tent camping spots, I noticed a lone figure, seated out on one of the narrow fishing piers. He was barely visible, blending with the shadows cast by the campground lights.

Changing direction, I headed toward the person, recognizing him as I drew near enough to see the light glinting off his auburn hair.

"Hey." I put my plate and utensils aside and sat down beside Rusty Mason. "How are you doing?"

"Not good." He crumpled up a can and I noticed that instead of a beer, he was drinking a soda. It reminded me that I needed to talk to him about his potentially fake ID. But not now. The man had lost his brother today, and grilling him about underage drinking wasn't appropriate at this time.

"I'm so sorry about your brother," I told him. "I know how it is to lose someone you love, someone that's family. But I can imagine this is worse because his passing was so sudden and unexpected."

Rusty let out a long, slow breath, then nodded. "It *was* unexpected. He was young, and I figured we'd all have fifty more years together. I can't wrap my head around him being gone. He was a total butt, and we didn't always get along, but he was my brother. He loved me, and I loved him."

A butt. I couldn't help but be amused, thinking that the descriptor was something a teenager would say.

"I wish I knew what happened," he continued. "I just want answers. Did he have a serious medical condition that he hid from us? That he ignored because he wanted to live life on his own terms? If so, I totally get that. That's what I want the autopsy to reveal. I don't want Paul to have died because he was taking drugs or because he and Peter got into a fight the night before. Peter is even more of a wreck than I am. He's drunk in the cabin right now, crying that it's his fault, that he should have turned back when Paul was sick, that if he'd come back with him, he could have called for help and Paul might still be alive."

I wanted to reassure him, but I wasn't sure what else I could say. Those autopsy results couldn't come soon enough. I knew these things took weeks in big cities, but the town was so small that the local coroner doubled as the ambulance medic. This had to be the only case Stef was working on. Were there labs she could do in-house? Did everything have to be sent to a larger town like Derwood, or even to Roanoke?

What would she find? That Paul had died of a heart attack, tragically young? That he'd overdosed and somehow managed to hide his drug habit from his brothers? What had happened to cause his death? And what was the white stuff on his sandwich?

"Did your brother take his blood thinner pills in the morning or in the evening?" I asked Rusty. "Was he someone who needed to chop his pills up and mix them with his food, or did he just swallow them with a drink?"

Maybe the white stuff on the sandwich remains were Paul's blood thinner pills and he'd done that as a way of ingesting them. Most adults I knew just swallowed them with a glass of water, but I remember I'd struggled with that in my early teens and had to take things like aspirin chopped up in a spoon full of applesauce.

It had tasted horrible, and I'd quickly mastered the art of swallowing pills, but I could imagine some people might always need to cut down and hide their medications.

Rusty shot me a perplexed look. "He took them in the morning. With his coffee. Just swallowing them like normal people do. Why?"

I shrugged. "Just wondering."

"Wondering why?" Rusty got to his feet. "Did you hear something about the autopsy? What did they find in his stomach? What's going on?"

I stood as well, facing him. "I don't know anything official."

"The deputy was asking about drug use. Is that what happened to him?" Rusty demanded. "Because Paul didn't take drugs. If they found drugs in his system, then someone put them in his food or drink or something."

Rusty opened his mouth to continue saying something, then shut it, a horrified expression flitting across his face.

"I'm not saying someone drugged your brother," I assured him. "Until we hear anything official, we should assume that he died of a heart attack or of some medical condition he hadn't wanted to share with you and Peter."

"Paul turned back on the trail because he was having stomach problems," Rusty said. "That's why he turned back. Not because he had chest pains."

"Heart attacks don't always come on like chest pains," I told him. "My grandfather died of one and he'd been complaining of indigestion and numbness in his arm. I'm not a doctor, Rusty. And neither are you. Let's wait for the police to finish their investigation before we let our imaginations run wild."

It was good advice, and I probably needed to heed it myself.

But I wouldn't, because this was my campground, I'd been the one to find Paul's body, and I felt somewhat guilty about his death. He'd died here, while on vacation at my business. As much as I hoped Paul had died from something that had nothing to do with the campground or my friends, that gnawing feeling in my stomach told me otherwise.

CHAPTER 16

I was up and at the office before sunrise, getting the coffee started and prepping for those early campers who wanted to grab a cup of joe or some snacks before heading out to fish.

The bell on the door rang and I turned around, expecting to see Sierra with the morning delivery. Instead I was surprised that it was Lottie coming through the doorway.

"You're back!" I went over and gave her a quick hug. "I didn't expect you until tomorrow. How's Amanda?"

She sighed. "My daughter has turned into Bridezilla. One minute she wants my help, and the next she wants me to go home. Is this wedding going to be in the church with two hundred guests, or will she and her fiancé elope to Vegas? It's anyone's guess right now."

"There's a lot to plan, and she *just* got engaged. I'm sure it's very stressful, trying to decide what she and her fiancé want," I replied.

As much as I wanted to sympathize with Lottie's daughter, I couldn't relate. My own wedding plans had been simple. I'd spent most of my working life organizing huge corporate events and trade shows. I didn't get the whole wedding-planning anxiety at all. And I was endlessly grateful that Colter and Greg hadn't stressed over their ceremony and reception.

"We'll talk about the dress fitting and cake tasting later." Lottie waved the topic away with a sweep of her hand. "I heard what happened and had to come see you first thing this morning. You found a *body*? As in, a *dead* body?"

I nodded. "A guest. Elvis led me to him. We were taking a hike and he pulled me onto a side trail to an overlook, and there he was. Oh, Lottie, it was so horrible to find him like that."

I told her everything, from the drunken bonfire antics to when I'd found Paul Mason. "I went around with Jake to interview the other guests. Until they determine cause of death, they're treating it as suspicious. But he was on blood thinners, and he'd been really drunk the night before. It's horrible that he died, but I'm hoping it was of natural causes."

"Well *I* heard that natural causes might not be what's on the coroner's report," Lottie said.

My eyes widened. "What did you hear? Was it from your brother's friend's cousin's girlfriend's buddy who works at the morgue?"

Lottie laughed. "Just a friend at the morgue. The cousin's girlfriend's brother's friend's buddy is the one at the sheriff's office."

"So, what did he or she say?"

"The dead man's blood tested positive for opiates. They're waiting for the lab to get back with the exact amount, but other evidence from the autopsy points to a drug overdose."

I frowned. "His brothers absolutely swear he was not a

drug user. Is that something people can hide? And I'm pretty sure Jake didn't find any drugs among Paul's belongings—other than the blood thinner medication he had in his glove box, that is."

"Maybe he kept his illegal narcotics in the blood thinner bottle, so no one would know," Lottie suggested. "As for hiding a drug from family members, I think it can happen if they aren't around all the time or if their friends and family are particularly oblivious. Just like some people are functional alcoholics, I think some people can be functional drug users."

"Until they're *not* functional," I pointed out, thinking that eventually either the expenses or the need to keep upping the dose to get the same high would catch up with a person.

"True," Lottie agreed.

"His brother Peter will be relieved that Paul didn't die from internal bleeding," I added. "Paul had been on blood thinners. He and Peter had gotten into a brawl the night before. According to the youngest brother, Rusty, Peter has been a wreck, thinking he killed Paul."

She shook her head. "I'm no expert, but I think if a fight had caused internal bleeding the guy would have been either dead or at the hospital and not going out for a hike the next morning."

"So, drugs," I mused. "Not a heart attack. Not Peter's fault. Just a guy who accidentally overdosed."

I was relieved…at least until I remembered the white stuff on the food.

"Could someone have drugged him without his knowledge?" I asked Lottie. "Chopped up the oxycodone or whatever and put it in his food or drink?"

Lottie wrinkled her nose. "I guess, but wouldn't that be horribly bitter? I'd think someone wouldn't get more than a tiny amount before they spit the food or drink out because it tasted horrible."

"What if they put it in something that was supposed to be bitter? Or something that was spicy and could cover up the taste?" I suggested.

"Like coffee?" She glanced over to where the coffee urn was perking away. "But if someone put drugs in your huge vat of coffee, half the campground would have overdosed."

"No, not in the camp store coffee." I waved the idea away. "Paul only drank decaf. The Masons made their coffee using the coffee maker in the cabin. And Paul had forgotten to bring his coffee, so Rusty, the youngest, ordered a special bag of decaf from The Coffee Dog. Rusty picked it up the morning before Paul died along with their food orders."

"Then we're back to one of the brothers being guilty," Lottie said. "They were the only ones who would have had access to the coffee between the time it was brewed and when the dead man drank it. So maybe the one who thought he'd killed his brother actually had? Or the younger one?"

I thought about that for a second. It didn't make sense. Why would Rusty have wanted his brother dead? And Peter might have motive, but he seemed absolutely devastated that Paul had died, and was blaming himself.

"No. If Peter had put a lethal dose of opiates in his brother's coffee, then I doubted he would have been so shocked at his death. And I would think he'd want to be more chill about the whole thing instead of crying to Rusty that he killed Paul by accident."

"Hmm. Maybe," Lottie said, not sounding convinced. "My money is still on this Peter guy. Man, why does all the interesting stuff happen when I'm away looking at five thousand dollar bridal gowns?"

"I'd rather the interesting stuff not happen," I replied.

"And back to the murder brainstorming session, I'm not sure it was the coffee. I...I think it might have been his sandwich."

Lottie's eyes widened. "His *sandwich*? Does he douse his sandwich with a quarter cup of fresh horseradish? Or tons of spicy Dijon? Because I can't see how someone could hide the bitter taste of crushed pills on a turkey and Swiss with mayo. Does he have a special mustard he always carries with him that this Peter could have doctored with the pills?"

I also noticed that Lottie hadn't mentioned that Sierra also would have means to dose both the coffee grounds and the sandwich before they were delivered. And I appreciated her friendship and loyalty. That made me decide I should confide in her and trust that she wouldn't spread this information around town. Sierra already had enough scrutiny without me adding to it.

"Paul was eating a grilled veggie lettuce wrap with extra sauce when he died," I told her.

"Ooo, I love those things!" Lottie exclaimed. "I can never get Sierra to give me the sauce recipe, no matter how much I badger her. You're right though. That spicy sauce might cover up the bitter taste of the pills. So you're suggesting Peter killed his brother by grinding up oxycodone and putting it in his grilled veggie wrap?"

"I don't think it was Peter," I told her. "There's something off there, but I don't think he murdered Paul. But I *do* think it was the sandwich. When I found the body, there were the remains of the sandwich right by his hand, along with a spilled thermos of coffee. The lettuce wrap had come off and I saw some white stuff in the sauce, like ground up pills."

"Or lumps of cornstarch for thickening." Lottie shook her head. "No, it couldn't be cornstarch. Sierra would have noticed. She never would send something out with cornstarch lumps in it. No, it was Peter. I know it."

She was absolutely fixated on Peter as the murderer, and I knew why.

"Peter and Rusty both would have had opportunity," I said, slowly working through my thought process. "Peter had motive—although I still don't think he did it. But Sierra also had both the opportunity and the motive."

"You don't seriously think Sierra *killed* someone?" Lottie shrieked. "No! I mean, I *could* totally see Sierra killing someone given the right circumstances, but she'd never sneak pills in their food—especially food coming from her own kitchen. Her establishment's reputation means too much to her. And she's not a sneaky killer. I'm pretty sure if Sierra wanted someone dead, she'd knife them. With one of those big kitchen knives."

Yikes.

"It wasn't Sierra," I assured her. "You're right. She'd never do that, and never ruin an amazing sandwich with crushed up pills." I suddenly realized something. "Plus it *couldn't* be her. Paul is the one she's angry with. The grilled veggie wrap was for *Rusty*, the youngest brother. His name was on the bag. She would have had no idea that Paul would eat the sandwich instead, and she doesn't want Rusty dead at all."

"You should be a lawyer, Sassy," Lottie said with an admiring smile.

"Thanks." I was on a roll here, and didn't have the mental space to do more than acknowledge the compliment.

"Even the coffee had Rusty's name on it," I continued. "It was for Paul, but Rusty had ordered it and I remember he put his name on the form. And I remember his name was on the bag."

"So whoever wanted Paul dead had to have doctored the sandwich after it was picked up by Rusty and out of the bag," Lottie mused. "Actually they would have had to doctor it after Rusty gave the sandwich to his brother. So we're back to Peter. Or Rusty."

"Or someone Paul came across on the trail when he turned back." I frowned. "He met another hiker. They both went to the overlook to have lunch and...I don't know. The other hiker doctored his sandwich while Paul went into the woods to pee?"

"That doesn't make sense," Lottie pointed out. "There's a whole lot of chance there. This killer is just carrying around crushed up pills just in case Paul turns around early and is hiking back alone? Just in case Paul agrees to go have lunch with him at a secluded overlook? Just in case Paul leaves his food open and unattended long enough for the guy to put the pills in it? And that his choice of luncheon sandwich has a spicy enough sauce to cover up the bitter taste of the pills?"

I held up my hands. "I hope the police are better at this than we are, because I've got nothing. No suspects with means, motive and opportunity. None."

"None except Peter." Lottie pursed her lips. "Maybe you should be looking at the 'means' part of the investigation. Who had access to drugs?"

"That could be anyone," I countered. "People get pills when they have their wisdom teeth out, or pull a muscle in their back. If there *is* a killer, the pills could have been theirs, or a family member's. People save those things. When Mom and I went through the medicine cabinet after Dad died, we found a bottle of Percocet from 1988."

"Well, call me if you find any more clues. Or stumble upon any more dead bodies." Lottie reached out and gave me another hug. "I'll be back later this afternoon, after a nap. I've got no idea how you get up this early every morning. I never would have hauled my butt over here if I hadn't been dying to know about the dead guy."

"Thanks?" I hugged her back, chuckling at how quirky my friend was.

Lottie headed toward the door, then stopped, turning her head to look back at me. "Oh! I almost forgot. There was another interesting thing my friend told me about the autopsy. It seems that Paul had taken some laxatives the day he'd died. Can you imagine? Laxatives, after a night of drinking? When you're hungover and probably pooping like crazy anyway? It just doesn't make sense."

CHAPTER 17

"*L*axatives," I repeated to myself as Lottie left.

Rusty had said that Paul had suffered from intestinal distress that morning. It was the reason he'd given for turning back on the trail.

"Why would Paul need to take laxatives when that case of beer and the whisky would have done the trick for him?" I asked Elvis. "Plus, why take laxatives then go off on a hike? He had to have known what would happen."

My hound stared at me with his dark, liquid eyes, then sighed and dropped his head back on his paws to return to his nap. I poured myself a cup of fresh coffee from the urn and sat down to think.

"Maybe Paul didn't take the laxatives. Maybe someone snuck them into his breakfast or something. People have been pranking others with laxatives since the things hit the drugstore shelves."

I thought of the white bits inside the sandwich Paul had eaten. Maybe that had been laxative pills and not opiates? But he hadn't had the sandwich until *after* he'd turned back and laxatives took hours to work. Besides, if the white stuff

150

on the sandwich was a chopped up laxative pill, then we were back to thinking the opiates were ground up in his coffee.

My head hurt trying to think through this tangled skein of pills, motives, and methods.

Getting up from the table, I poured myself another cup of coffee. I might not be able to figure out who killed Paul Mason, but I had a good hunch on who might have dosed him with a laxative.

The sky was just beginning to lighten in anticipation of sunrise when Sierra burst through the door, a box in her hands.

"Sorry! I'm so sorry I'm late." She put the box on the table, organizing the bags with the breakfast and lunch orders. "I didn't get to sleep until around two this morning and over-slept my four o'clock alarm. I'd still be in bed if Deshaun hadn't woken me up."

"It's okay. None of the guests have been by yet for their food orders, so we're good. Does any of that need to go in the fridge?" I asked.

She held up a bag. "I'm separating those out right now. You go on with what you were doing. I'll take care of this."

I hesitated a second, but had to ask. "Sierra, did you put anything in Rusty Mason's food order? Or the bag of decaf coffee? I wouldn't really blame you given what his brother did."

Her eyes widened. "No! I'd never do that. Never! And why would I want to hurt Rusty? He saved my daughter. I owe him. If I was going to poison someone, it would be Paul."

"I believe you," I assured her. "But I just want—"

"Oh no. Was there something in his food?" she inter-rupted. "Is that what killed him? Sassy, I swear to you I would never do something like that. My food, my business, my reputation...it means everything to me. I don't care if I had to make a sandwich for a convicted serial killer, I would never do something like that. I'd yell at him. Maybe punch him. But I'd never dose his food. Never."

I held up my hands. "I didn't think you did it, Sierra. I just had to ask. When I found Paul's body he had part of a sandwich spilled next to him and there was something in it—something that looked like crushed-up pills. And I heard the coroner found opiates in his system."

"Opiates? Where the heck would I get opiates? All we've got in the house is Tylenol." Sierra gasped. "They think I did it. They think I killed him, don't they?"

"I don't know for sure if that's what killed him or if the stuff on the sandwich even was oxycodone. And it was on *Rusty's* sandwich. You had no way of knowing Paul was going to eat Rusty's sandwich."

I shouldn't have said anything. All I'd done is upset and worry her further.

"I'm going to be arrested," Sierra said in a stoic tone of voice. "Guess I better find a good lawyer. Sassy, if you get called in to testify at my trial, I don't want you to lie. Go ahead and tell them I was arguing with Paul Thursday night. And that I've been delivering the food, that the guest names are on the order form so it would have been easy for me to know which sandwich was his."

"The names are on the bags too," I pointed out. "And they're right here out in the open in the box or in the fridge. Guests come in and pick out the bag with their name on it, and leave. Lots of times they open up the bag and unwrap the sandwich, just to check and make sure it's what they ordered. We get busy. We might not notice if someone unwrapped a sandwich, sprinkled something on it, then put it back and grabbed another bag. Someone else could have easily done this—including his own brothers. They were sharing a place together, and one had a brawl with Paul in front of the cabin.

Another camper witnessed it. They could have put something in the sandwich while Paul was showering or something."

Sierra straightened her shoulders. "I'll be sure to tell my lawyer that. Maybe it'll be enough for reasonable doubt."

"Stop with the lawyer thing. I'm sorry I even asked you." I reached out to give her a quick hug. "First, the pills I saw were on Rusty's sandwich. Like I said, you had no idea Paul would eat Rusty's food, and you had no reason to want Rusty dead. Second, for all we knew Paul was secretly a drug addict and overdosed all by himself. You're not going to jail."

"I hope not." She swiped a hand under her eyes and a determined expression settled on her face. "I need to do a better job at controlling my temper."

"Are you kidding me? If someone had done that to my child, no one would have found the body," I joked. Well, kinda joked. "I'm going to find out what happened to Paul Mason. I trust the police—well, I trust Jake Bailey, I'm not so sure about the sheriff or the other deputy since I haven't spent a whole lot of time with either of them. Anyway, I trust the police are going to do their job, but this is *my* campground and you are *my* friend. Both are affected by this death, and I'm not going to sit around and wait while someone else investigates."

Sierra chuckled. "Somehow that's not a surprise. I'd offer to help, but I'm thinking it's probably best for me to stay as far away from the investigation as possible."

"True," I agreed. "But there are a few things we can do right now. I'm a bit alarmed at the idea that someone could have tampered with another guest's food and we might not have noticed. Starting now, the food box is going behind the counter and the stuff that needs cooling is going in the storeroom fridge."

Sierra grimaced. "You and your mom are going to need to

go get people's orders for them. No more grab-and-go. It'll mean extra time for you and your guests who might be in a hurry."

"But it'll mean I can assure them no one has messed with their food," I countered. "The grab-and-go system worked great when we had all of six guests here. With a full camp-ground, we need to change things."

She nodded. "Do you want to keep the names off the orders? Do numbers and have a list to cross reference or something."

"Heck no." I didn't even have to think about that one. "It's quicker if their names are on the bag and I trust you and your business, Sierra. We might want to eventually go with some kind of online ordering system, though."

"That would be easier if the orders keep growing like they have, but I know Flora will miss coming by here in the evenings."

I smiled. "I'll miss her too, but it'll be summer soon. Let her know when she drops the morning food off, she's welcome to stay and hike or swim or sunbathe. I can even reserve a kayak for her if she'd like to do some paddling or fishing."

"I'll definitely let her know." Sierra smiled. "But I don't want her spending her whole summer lying on a dock by the lake. She's gonna have regular hours at the coffee shop if she hasn't found another job. And there's the whole college-thing to think about as well. Hopefully she'll change her mind about that."

I nodded, but my sympathies were with Flora on this one. I was a parent. I'd been there. I understood Sierra's concerns about college and her daughter's future. But life was short and spending a teenage summer kayaking or sunning by the lake? That was the stuff memories were made of.

CHAPTER 18

There was some confusion during the morning rush about my changed policy on food order retrieval. People would come in, walk to where the box of food orders formerly sat, then stare at the empty table for an amusingly long period of time. Then they would look around the store, identical perplexed expressions on their faces, before wandering to the counter to ask where the food was. It would have been funny if I hadn't been so busy racing around that I didn't have time to appreciate the humor.

I sorted out everyone's breakfast and lunch deliveries in between sales of snacks, drinks, and bait, six canoe and kayak rentals, and the distribution of a dozen trail maps. When mom arrived at ten to take over for me, the rush had passed and the last customer had just left after picking up a bag of venison jerky and a bottle of Gatorade.

"That young woman with the camper van just stopped me out front to tell me that there's a fight in front of the cabins by the blue-blaze trail entrance," Mom said before even wishing me a good morning.

My heart skipped a beat, my mind immediately going

back to the fight late Friday night between Paul Mason and his brother Peter. But Paul was dead. Was it Rusty and Peter fighting this time? It had to be them. The only other occupied cabins by the trail entrance were the one the painter with the Doritos was renting, and the one Jimmie Free was staying at. Jimmie had gone fishing at seven this morning, and I couldn't see Denver Twigg getting into a fight, so it had to be Rusty and Peter Mason.

"She said it was some man arguing with a woman, and she wouldn't normally have said anything, but the guy is really loud.

Adelaide. I'd given her the key to cabin eleven, which was next to Jimmie Free's cabin and directly across from the Masons' cabin. She must have decided to move either late last night or this morning, and Charlie was upset over her decision.

"Come on Elvis," I called, rousing the bloodhound from where he was sleeping behind the counter. Elvis wasn't all that good of a guard dog, but he was huge and had a low growly-bark that was very intimidating. If I needed to deal with an angry man this morning, I wanted the bloodhound by my side.

"Food orders are behind the counter and in the storeroom fridge," I called out to mom as Elvis and I ran for the door. "I'll explain later."

Grabbing Elvis's leash, I clipped it on his collar then jogged toward the line of cabins. Thankfully the argument wasn't quite as loud as I'd been imagining, and the only crowd of spectators was the painter, the two Mason brothers, and Shelane, who had a daypack on her back and a wooden walking stick in her hand. From the intent expression on her face, I got the impression the woman was debating whether she should intervene or not.

I was actually glad she was there, not only because she

looked completely capable of beating down Charlie with that stick, but because it was good to have another un-involved woman here besides me.

Adelaide stood on the porch of the cabin, her hands on her hips. The door was open, and behind her Lexi cowered, eyes wide.

"This is ridiculous," Charlie ranted. "Come back to the camper." The man waved his hands, taking a few frustrated steps in each direction, but not approaching the cabin. He was a good twenty feet away from his wife, which no doubt accounted for the yelling. But the distance reassured me that he wasn't planning anything physical.

"No." Adelaide's chin lifted. "Grilling Lexi about who I've been talking to? Going through my phone in the middle of the night and reading my text messages? Accusing me of…" She shot an embarrassed glance toward the two Mason brothers, "…of being unfaithful? I'm done Charlie. You either trust me or you don't. And if you don't, then there's nothing left of this marriage."

"How am I supposed to trust you when you keep secrets from me?"

Adelaide flinched at that. "Some secrets aren't mine to tell, Charlie. And some secrets don't have anything to do with us, my relationship with you, or this marriage."

My eyebrows shot up at that. I'd been blaming Charlie for this whole thing, but I'd only heard Adelaide's point of view. I'd trusted in what she'd told me and my own, probably biased, observations. But she'd just said she'd been keeping secrets.

Everyone kept secrets. From that purchase hidden from a spouse to an occasional white lie, everyone kept secrets.

My husband had kept secrets too, and I'd been absolutely blindsided when he'd confessed to the affair and asked for a divorce. I hadn't been the only one shocked by his revelation.

Our friends, our families, had all thought we had a loving and solid marriage. It had rocked me, made me feel an absolute fool for thinking everything was roses and sunshine while my husband had been falling in love with another. Decades later, I still distrusted my ability to "see the signs." It was probably one of the reasons I'd never done more than date casually after my divorce—and eventually had given up on even that.

Friends and family I welcomed into my heart, but when it came to romance, I just couldn't trust—couldn't trust either myself or any of the men I felt a spark of attraction toward. Charlie's mention of secrets and Adelaide's admission that there were things she'd kept from him, dredged all the hurt from the depths of my past to sit raw and painful on the surface of my heart.

"Fine. Just fine. Stay here, then. It'll be easier for you to screw around." Charlie waved a hand toward the Mason brothers. "Right across from your lover. No wonder you picked this cabin. Don't think I don't know what you've been doing, Adelaide. You both might try to hide it, but I know."

For a second I wondered if he could possibly be right. Peter had a confused expression his face. Rusty looked mortified, though, and I wasn't sure if it was because he'd been caught or because the idea of sleeping with a married woman embarrassed him. He was a good-looking guy, but a good bit younger than Adelaide. No, it had to just be Charlie's irrational jealousy talking. I couldn't see Adelaide as the type of woman to hook up with a random younger man at a campground right under the nose of her jealous husband and her curious six-year-old daughter.

Adelaide's face reddened. "I can talk to people, Charlie. It's not against our marriage vows to talk to people."

My eyebrows shot up. Charlie had caught her talking to Rusty? I'm assuming it was Rusty since the young man's face was just as red as Adelaide's at this point. But Adelaide was right, it wasn't against her marriage vows to talk to someone.

"For the last time, Charlie, I'm not having an affair," Adelaide insisted. "You need to trust me. Those e-mails…you just need to trust me and stop this nonsense."

E-mails? What e-mails? Clearly there was more to this whole thing than Adelaide had let on.

"Trust you?" Charlie scoffed. "Like you trust me? You can't trust me enough to tell me why you're secretly talking to a man you're *not* having an affair with, even if it sure sounds like that from the e-mails, but I'm supposed to trust *you*?"

The man spun around and stalked off, heading back toward the RV sites. Shelane's grip on the stick loosened. Adelaide put her hands over her face, while Lexi clung to her legs.

"What a nutjob," Peter Mason muttered as he and his brother headed back inside.

Denver came toward me. "I thought having those brothers brawling in the middle of the night was bad enough, but now I've got a woman with an angry estranged husband for a neighbor.

"I'm so sorry," I told the man. "I'd be happy to give you a voucher for a free night next time you stay with us."

Hopefully he would stay with us again. I'd done everything to make this campground the perfect vacation spot, but ultimately there was so much out of my control. Mom was right. I needed to stop fretting over the things I couldn't change, over a future I couldn't predict, and take time each day to appreciate what I had.

And to appreciate that what I had was another day. There was no guarantee of a future at all, and that made each sunrise, each hike, each moment precious beyond belief. I couldn't let the marital problems of guests, or the suspicious death of another guest ruin my appreciation of this gift I'd been given—the gift of more time.

Denver shrugged. "Disruption isn't always a bad thing. I used to rent a cabin out in the middle of the woods with no one around for miles. Do you know how much painting I got done? A lot. But I was lonely, and I found that those paintings lacked a special something. Conflict, the messy business of rubbing elbows on a day-to-day basis with our fellow humans is what brings art to life. So here I am, disrupted, annoyed, but alive and producing some of my best paintings." He turned to look at the cabin kitty-corner from his. "And I've got a soft spot for kids. Do you think it would be okay if I offered to let the little girl paint with me today? It would give her mom and dad some time to think or talk, and it might do the kid some good to work out her own feelings on canvas."

I glanced over at Adelaide and Lexi, then back to Denver. "I think she'd like that. She's a really sweet girl, and she's enjoyed the crafts we've done this week."

Just when I was thinking everything was falling apart, here was someone who was reaching out and helping instead of slamming the campground online. I hoped the other campers felt the same.

But what a soap opera this week had turned out to be. Drunk and rowdy guests. A dead man. A marriage imploding right before our eyes.

Charlie and Adelaide's issue wasn't the most important problem I needed to deal with, though. Paul Mason had died because someone had slipped him drugs.

Frowning, I wondered something. Was the crime because someone wanted Paul dead, or because someone wanted Sierra in jail for murder? Maybe I was going at this all wrong. When Sierra stopped by tonight for the food orders, I'd need to ask her if there was anyone in town who'd benefit if she went to jail, or if her business was ruined because the town thought her a murderer.

In spite of my emotion-felt pledge of Sierra, I was in no position to be investigating a man's murder. There was too much I didn't know, too many things going on in people's backgrounds that I couldn't bring to light.

Too many secrets.

Anyone in this campground could be the killer. Or it could be someone outside the campground that hadn't cared who ended up dead as long as Sierra was blamed for it. It was a bit scary to look around and wonder who might be the murderer in our midst, so instead I decided to deal with a lesser crime.

Two brothers had brawled over Paul sleeping with Peter's wife, and while Rusty had said they'd done the whole forgive-and-forget routine, I somehow doubted Peter would have just let it go that easy. I couldn't imagine Peter deliberately murdering his brother, but I could definitely see him wanting to punish him for what he'd done via an unpleasant and uncomfortable method. It was a prank that teens and college kids had been performing forever, and I could absolutely see one of the Mason brothers resorting to it.

I was pretty sure that Paul hadn't ingested a laxative knowingly, not after a night of drunkenness and a planned hike through the woods. Someone had slipped him the pill— or the chocolate square. And I can imagine that giving his brother a case of the runs seemed like a small amount of payback for what Paul had done.

I left Denver and Adelaide and Lexi, and walked across the gravel to cabin ten.

CHAPTER 19

*R*usty answered at my knock, his brow furrowing with worry when he saw me.

"I didn't sleep with her," he blurted out. "I was just talking to her. That's it."

"I'm not here about that," I assured him. "Can I come in for a second?"

He hesitated. "Look, I know we haven't been your best guests, but Paul died. It's not like we're going to be partying it up after that. We might drown our sorrows, but we'll do it in the peace of our own cabin. Peter and I won't be any trouble."

"Not trouble like psycho-jealous guy anyway," Peter called from inside the cabin.

"I know you won't be any trouble. And I'm so sorry for your loss. I found something out this morning about Paul, and that's what I wanted to talk to you both about."

Rusty opened the door wide and ushered me in. I entered the cabin, noting that it looked very much like it had yesterday when Jake and I had been here. There was no sign of Jake's investigation, no difference other than the fact that

Paul's belongings had been packed up and set neatly to the side.

Peter stood by the chair and small table that held a selection of books from the main house. My eyes met his, and I flinched slightly at the sound of Rusty closing the cabin door firmly behind me. I would have been unnerved being in here with two men, one of whom might be a murderer, except for the fact that I didn't think either man had killed his brother. Well, and the fact that I still had Elvis by my side. The hound was a lover, not a fighter, but I had no doubt that if things got ugly, he'd defend me.

"You found something out about Paul's death?" Rusty asked, walking around to stand next to Peter. "Was it his heart? Did he fall and hit his head? What happened?"

"The coroner hasn't released a report yet, but I heard from a reliable source that they found laxatives in his system." I waited a few seconds to let that bit of information land, watching the two men carefully. Rusty seemed perplexed. Peter's expression was unchanged.

"It seems odd that someone would take a laxative right before a big hike," I commented. "Especially after having drank heavily the night before. It's been a long time since I was more than slightly tipsy, but I remember having the opposite problem after a night of drinking."

"No!" Rusty spun to look at his brother. "You didn't! Peter, that's stupid stuff kids do, not grown men."

Peter's face crumpled. "It wasn't...I didn't.... It was a joke. I just was getting back at him for sleeping with Hope. I loved Paul. I was mad at him, but I loved him. He was my brother and I never wanted anything to happen to him besides a bad case of the runs. We fought. I got it out of my system. I'd forgiven him. This was just my last punch before I let it all go. I never meant for him to die. Did I kill him? Was it my fault? Oh God, I don't think I can live with myself if it's my fault that he died."

I don't know what I'd expected, but this outpouring of raw emotion and guilt surprised me. And from the expression on Rusty's face, it surprised him too.

The younger brother turned to me, his eyes wide. "Is that what killed Paul? Did he...poop himself to death or something? Was it his heart problems or other medication that reacted with the laxatives? Because people did that kind of thing all the time in high school and college and no one ever died before. They were darned uncomfortable for a day, but that was it. I never would have believed laxatives could kill a person, and I'm sure Peter didn't know that or he never would have given them to Paul."

Suddenly I wasn't sure what to do. I hadn't expected a heartfelt confession or Rusty pleading Peter's case for him. I was in over my head, and for once I had the sense to call in someone who might actually be better than me at handling this situation.

I pulled my phone from my pocket, eyeing the two men with some trepidation, then looking at Elvis who was sprawled at my feet, tongue lolling out with relaxed cheerfulness. If the dog wasn't worried about our safety, then maybe I didn't need to be either.

"You really should talk to the police about this," I said to Pete as I punched the redial for Jake's number. "It might have nothing to do with your brother's death, but the police still need to know so they can factor it in to their investigation."

I wasn't sure what Peter's reaction would be, and was a bit relieved to see he didn't argue against my suggestion. If anything, he seemed to agree with me, dropping into the chair and nodding as he swept a hand over his face.

"I do need to let the police know," Peter said. "If I killed my brother, I'm prepared to pay for that crime. I didn't mean to do it. I never wanted to really harm him. But if I caused his death, then I should pay for my crimes."

The phone beeped as it dialed, and I held it up to my ear. Jake answered right away and didn't ask any questions when I requested he come down and meet me at cabin ten. As he hung up, I got paranoid that no one besides me and Rusty had heard Peter's confession, so I quickly texted the details to both Jake and my mother, then shoved the phone back in my pocket.

Elvis yawned, clearly not worried about any of this. His nonchalance gave me courage.

It took Jake ten minutes to get down the mountain and to the cabin. It seriously was one of the longest and most awkward ten minutes of my life. Peter sat in the chair, his head in his hands. Rusty paced around, clearly trying to avoid looking at either his brother or me. Elvis took a nap and started to snore. I fidgeted.

Relief washed through me when I heard Jake's knock on the cabin door. Rusty opened it and as he came in, his gaze swept the room, settling on me.

"What happened?"

"I killed Paul," Peter choked out. "I didn't mean to. I just wanted to get back at him for sleeping with Hope. I didn't know he was going to *die*."

"It's not his fault," Rusty added. "How was he supposed to know laxatives would kill Paul? They need to put warning labels on the bottle or something. They shouldn't be selling the stuff if there's a chance of someone dying."

"It was just a prank," Peter added. "But if I hadn't done it, he might be alive today. I had to go and slip him the laxative thinking an epic case of the runs was what he deserved. I killed my own brother."

Jake listened to all of this with an admirably straight face.

But when he turned to look at me, I saw the bewilderment in his eyes.

"I heard from a source that the coroner found laxatives in Paul's system," I explained, hoping that Lottie had been right and that I hadn't dragged Jake down here to hear a confession of a prank that had no bearing on the case whatsoever.

I could tell Jake was fighting an eye-roll. But instead of raking me over the coals for wasting his time, he took out his notepad and walked over to Peter.

"Tell me exactly what happened. Start from when you found out that your brother was sleeping with your estranged wife."

Peter said that Paul had drunkenly confessed Friday night. He'd swung the first punch. "We took it outside because there's not a lot of room in here, and neither of us was so drunk that we were willing to risk our security deposit by wrecking the place," he explained. "The fight wasn't that bad. Lots of grappling and body punches, but that was it. We're brothers. We might be mad at each other, but neither of us wanted to seriously injure the other."

"When did you decide to slip your brother laxatives?" Jake asked.

Peter scrubbed a hand over his face and choked back a sob. "After the fight. We'd stopped because we were both drunk and tired, but Paul never apologized. He'd admitted to sleeping with Hope. Said it was just the one time and it was her coming on to him. That might have been true, but he's my *brother*. He knew I didn't want this divorce, that I was trying to get back together with Hope. How could he do that to me? How could he not even be sorry? I got the feeling if she showed up at his house one night, he'd do it again, and that made me angry. We shook hands, agreed to let it go, but I couldn't let it go. In the morning when Paul was sleeping, I got out some laxative powder then mixed it in a Gatorade bottle. Paul always drinks a bottle of Gatorade when he wakes up after a night of drinking. I figured it would kick in after a few hours when we were hiking."

"You always take laxatives camping with you?" Jake asked.

Peter hesitated, then nodded. "Yeah. Sometimes a change in food or different water binds me up a bit. It was just a prank. The guys at college used to do it all the time and no one died. I didn't expect him to die. I'm going to be in jail for the rest of my life, aren't I?"

"Did you add anything else to your brother's food or drink?" Jake asked. "Maybe pills? In his trail mix or sandwich? Did you switch out his heart pills for something else?"

Peter's eyes widened. "No. Just the laxative powder. I didn't want to kill Paul. I didn't want to even seriously hurt him. I just wanted to make him uncomfortable for the day as payback for what he did."

Jake turned to Rusty. "How about you? Any paybacks on your end I need to know about?"

Rusty shook his head. "No. This was between Peter and Paul. I didn't agree with what Paul did, but it wasn't my place to punish Paul for anything. I broke up the fight, told them both to let it all go. If I had known what Peter was planning with the laxative, I would have talked him out of it. And if I'd seen him putting stuff in Paul's bottle or coffee, I would have intervened and tossed it all out."

Jake closed his notepad and stuck it back in his pocket along with the pen.

"Are you gonna arrest me?" Peter repeated.

"Not right now," Jake told him. "Rumors aside, those laxatives didn't kill your brother. But he had ingested a substantial amount of Oxycodone. I need to ask once more if your brother was taking prescription pain medicine either legally or illegally."

Both men shook their heads.

"He wasn't an addict," Rusty said in a firm tone of voice. "He didn't even take aspirin. His heart pills were it."

"Wait, did someone swap out narcotics for his heart pills?" Peter asked. "Someone killed Paul, didn't they? Someone drugged him and killed him. I'll bet it was the woman from the coffee shop. She threatened Paul last year, and he said she accosted him Thursday night behind the camp store and threatened him again."

I flinched at the mention of Sierra's name, and noticed that Rusty did as well.

"That woman threatened him," Peter said. "She threatened him last year, and Paul said she'd confronted him this year as well. Is she the one that killed him? Was it her?"

"I've known Sierra a long time, and I can't imagine her a killer, but then people surprise me sometimes," Jake said. "You two have any idea what exactly that misunderstanding last year was about?"

Rusty was carefully studying the floor, his hands balled into fists at his side. Even Peter looked away.

"No. No idea," Peter replied, his voice flat. "Maybe he got drunk and peed on her building or her delivery van or something. That's probably what happened."

That was not what happened. I glared at Peter. "Well if people start thinking Sierra killed your brother, then she might have to actually tell people what happened last year. I know she doesn't want to do that, but she might end up without much of a choice."

Jake shot me a puzzled look, then turned his attention back to the Mason brothers. "What happened? Did he make a rude comment? Grab her butt? Insult her coffee or sandwiches?"

"I don't know what happened between them, but it wasn't a big deal as far as Paul was concerned," Peter said. "And it wasn't her food. We all love those sandwiches."

Rusty remained silent, staring at the floor.

"So neither of you were with Paul when whatever occurred between them last year?" Jake pressed. "Neither of you have any idea at all what happened to make Sierra Sanchez-Blue so mad at your brother?"

"No, sir," they both muttered in unison.

Jake closed his notebook. "Call me if you suddenly remember anything—anything about what happened last year, or about other altercations Paul may have gotten into with people in town, or at the campground. Anyone at all who might have wanted your brother dead."

"The only one who wanted him dead was that coffee shop woman," Peter snapped. "If someone killed my brother, then it was her. It was Sierra Sanchez-Blue."

CHAPTER 20

"I'm gonna make an educated guess here and say that you know what happened between Sierra and Paul Mason last year," Jake said as we left the Masons' cabin.

I bit my lip, wanting to tell him, wanting him to know the horrible thing that Paul had done.

"It's not my secret to tell," I finally said. And then I realized that was the same thing Adelaide had said to her husband. I'd faulted her for keeping secrets, and here I was doing the same thing—to a law enforcement officer too.

"I can respect that, especially since we clearly have someone, or multiple someone's in town who can't seem to keep a secret even if their job depended on it," he commented wryly.

"It's a small town. Hard to keep secrets in a small town." I was suddenly nervous, wondering if my confronting the Masons meant Lottie's friend at the coroner's office would lose their job.

"So, please tell me you don't really believe that Paul Mason pooped himself to death because his brother slipped him laxative powder, no matter how reliable this 'source' of yours is," Jake commented.

I blew out a breath. "No, I didn't believe that. I've got no idea who would have murdered Paul with a bunch of narcotics, but I had a pretty good idea who gave him a laxative. So I went for the low-hanging fruit, investigatively speaking."

"Low-hanging fruit is not any kind of investigation speak," Jake countered.

"Wait." I glanced over at him. "*Can* someone poop themselves to death? Is that a thing?"

"That's a question you'll need to ask Stef. Or Google." He sighed. "Look, I know you're friends with Lottie and she seems to know everything that goes on in this town, so I'm guessing that's your source. Don't worry. I'm not going to drive over and yell at her or anything, but I am gonna yell at you. Sassy, a man died yesterday—a man who was a guest at your campground."

"I know. And that's why—"

"It was initially called a suspicious death," Jake continued, interrupting me. "Which means there was a good chance someone murdered him. And now that the preliminary report from the coroner is in, it is official. Someone murdered Paul Mason. Although I'm going to do my job and pursue all leads, I don't think it was Sierra Sanchez-Blue. That means you might have a murderer here at your campground."

The thought sent a chill through me. Of course I'd considered there might be a murderer at the campground, but I'd been thinking in terms of non-premeditated, accidental manslaughter kind of thing. Not a murderer-murderer. I remembered when Lucky Miller had held a knife to my throat, demanding to know where a book he believed to be worth millions was, and shivered. That man had killed Daryl Butts, the campground handyman. He would have killed me. He had been a murderer-murderer. And I never wanted to meet one of those types ever again.

"I really don't want to get another phone call that has me driving a hundred miles an hour down a mountain to find Lottie straddling a duct-taped man with you standing over him holding a tire iron."

"It was a wrench," I corrected Jake.

He put a hand on my shoulder, ignoring my comment. "And I especially don't want to come tearing down the mountain to find that I'm too late, that you've been hurt. That you've been killed."

"I don't want that either." I blinked away sudden tears. I'd cheated death once, twice if I counted the guy who'd had a knife at my throat. There was only so much luck a person could have, and Jake's words made me think long and hard that I might have reached the end of mine. I wasn't a cat with nine-lives. The police would find who killed Paul Mason. My job needed to be making sure my non-dead guests had a wonderful vacation, and keeping myself from becoming a target of a murderer.

"Okay," I told Jake. Then I decided that I needed to clarify what exactly I was agreeing to, because although I might be a little shaken and scared now, my nosy, curious self might decide otherwise in a few days, or a few hours, or even a few minutes. "If I discover anything, I'll call you. I won't go running to confront anyone."

"Good." He paused by the porch steps to the camp store. "Now I need to see if you still have a list of the food delivery order from yesterday. Can I get a copy of that?"

I nodded. "Absolutely. It was the grilled veggie wrap, wasn't it? I saw the white powdery stuff on the sandwich that was by Paul Mason's body. When I found out he'd died from an opiate overdose, I knew that's what I saw on the food."

Jake looked heavenward mumbling something under his

breath, but he didn't comment further. I looped Elvis's leash around the porch railing and we went into the camp store. Pulling out yesterday's order form from the filing cabinet in the little back office area, I made Jake a copy and handed it over.

"It wasn't Sierra," I told Jake as he looked over the form. "The only thing on that order with Paul's name on it was the roast-beef sandwich—which he never ate because he left it behind at the cabin. The grilled veggie wrap with lettuce and extra sauce that was found by the body? That was Rusty's. He gave it to his brother when Paul turned back on the trail. Sierra would never want Rusty dead, and she would have no way of knowing that he was going to give his sandwich to Paul."

"So either Rusty killed his brother, or Peter did it after taking Paul's original sandwich from his pack because he knew Rusty would give his sandwich to Paul," Jake mused.

"That's a huge risk to take," I pointed out. "He could have killed the wrong brother. Plus, wouldn't it be easier to just put the pills on the roast beef? There's enough fresh horse-radish sauce on there to hide the pills and cover up the bitter taste."

"And then there's the idea that Paul might not have been the intended victim. Maybe the murderer has a thing against Sierra and is trying to frame her. Or maybe Rusty was the one who was supposed to die." He glanced around the store. "Tell me your process with these food deliveries. Do you give the bags to each camper as they come in each morning?"

I grimaced. "We do now. We used to put a box out on that table, and put the items that needed to be kept cold in that fridge with the sodas. People got their own orders. It wasn't a good system. It was just a matter of time until someone grabbed the wrong sandwich and I'd have to refund money to upset guests. When I suspected someone might have put something in Paul's sandwich, I changed our process."

He nodded. "Do you think you can make a list of who came in to pick up their food before the Masons' came to collect their order?"

I raised both hands. "I can try, but honestly we're really busy in the mornings. People who are planning to fish want to set out early and so do the hikers. We get a little rush between six and seven."

"Your best guess on who was here before him would really help," Jake said. "When exactly did Rusty come in to get the food?"

I frowned. "Mom came in early, at nine, to take over, and Rusty had been here before she'd arrived. Eight? Maybe seven thirtyish?"

Jake nodded. "Make a list and text it to me. Not just people picking up food orders, but others as well. Someone might have tampered with the sandwich while you were ringing someone else up."

"Or it could have been one of his brothers," I pointed out.

"They *are* the likeliest suspects," Jake agreed. "Rusty picked up the food. He would have had ample opportunity to add the pills before he took the food to the cabin. Then all he needs to do is take Paul's original sandwich out of his pack, then offer his own food to his brother when he agreed to turn back."

I couldn't imagine Rusty was the type of person to murder his brother, but I tried to look at it objectively. "Peter's laxative thing might have ruined the whole plan. Instead of eating lunch with them, Paul turned back. For all Rusty knew Paul wouldn't eat the sandwich at all and his opportunity would have passed. You didn't find any pills in the cabin, so he probably used all the ones he had. But Paul rallied, ate the sandwich, and collapsed alone in the middle of nowhere, far from any helpful hiker who might be carrying NARCAN."

"And he would have totally gotten away with it if it hadn't been for that pesky woman with her bloodhound and her gossipy friend," Jake intoned.

"Yeah. Those pesky kids." I laughed, impressed by his *Scooby-Doo* reference.

"Of course there's motive," Jake said with a shrug. "Peter has the motive, while Rusty has the opportunity. Maybe they did it together. Or maybe it was someone else. We have no proof that either of them had access to oxycodone."

"Oh I'm sure Deputy Sean is hard at work on that. Someone in that family had a wisdom tooth out or a pulled back muscle at one time or another, and kept the extra pills in a drawer somewhere."

"Everyone has skeletons in their closets and narcotics in their dresser drawers," he informed me, his lips twitching.

Then Jake folded the copy of the food order and stuck it in the back pocket of his jeans. He faced me, his expression suddenly sober. "Be careful, Sassy. And if you think someone's a murderer, please call me before barging into their cabin and confronting them."

I nodded, even though I hadn't barged into Peter and Rusty's cabin, and I hadn't considered them to be murderers. Not that I was convinced they were now, evidence or not. But Jake was right. I needed to be more careful.

Jake left and I looked down at the official copy of yesterday's order form as I walked back to the filing cabinet. Had Rusty doctored his own sandwich, knowing his brother might be especially hungry and that he'd eat the wrap if Rusty offered it to him? But Rusty didn't seem like a killer.

Not that I was any expert on killers. Maybe Rusty was one of those psychopaths that after being arrested for murder all his neighbors and co-workers would express shock and surprise. That was definitely chilling, but I couldn't imagine who else would have known Paul would be eating Rusty's sandwich. None of the other brothers had gotten sick. It had to be Rusty who'd put something in the sandwich. The only person who'd known that Paul was going to eat the veggie wrap was Rusty.

Unless...

Jake had thrown out there that Rusty might have been the intended victim. I hadn't thought too much about that at the time other than as a reason for Sierra's innocence but it made more sense for Rusty to have been the target all along, and Paul's death unintentional. Who would want Rusty dead, though? Not Sierra. She was grateful that he'd intervened and helped Flora last year.

Charlie? Would he attempt to murder someone he suspected of sleeping with Adelaide? It seemed so far-fetched. Wouldn't he go after e-mail guy rather than a random man at a campground that had only exchanged a few words with his wife? Even if she'd flirted a little, that hardly felt like enough motive for murder. Plus Charlie didn't seem like the type to carry around a bottle of narcotics, especially when his daughter would be camping with them.

Was it Peter? It would make his grief and guilt over Paul's death even more real if he'd planned to kill one brother and accidentally murdered the other. But what could Rusty have done to make Peter want to kill him? Surely if Peter was going to kill one of his brothers it would have been the one who slept with his wife.

What if Rusty *was* the killer? Maybe Paul slept with Rusty's girlfriend just like he'd done with Peter's wife and Rusty hadn't reacted by throwing punches and slipping laxatives into his older brother's drink.

I really needed to leave this to the police to figure out. I dug my phone out of my pocket, wondering if I should text

Jake my thoughts. I hated to be one of those people who tried to tell a trained officer how to do his job. I'd look like an annoying idiot micromanaging an investigation with absolutely no background in law enforcement.

I stuck the phone back in my pocket and put the order form back in the filing cabinet. I'd just shut the cabinet drawer when Mom came into the camp store.

"Did someone need to buy something?" she asked. "I took a quick break."

"There weren't any customers," I told her. "Don't feel guilty for needing a break. I was gone longer than I thought I'd be."

I went on to tell her everything, from my confronting the Mason brothers about the alleged laxative dosing, to Jake's and my suspicions concerning Rusty Mason as either the killer or the intended victim.

"First, I agree with Jake that you need to be more careful," Mom scolded. "Sassafras Louise, what were you thinking going into that cabin with two men, one or both of whom might have been a murderer?"

"I had Elvis with me," I explained, feeling as if I were an eight-year-old child and not a woman approaching sixty. "And I thought I was just confronting them over a prank. I didn't believe either of those men to be an actual murderer."

Mom narrowed her eyes and waved a finger at me. "You still need to be more careful. Two men against you and Elvis? I don't like that one bit, Sassy."

"So maybe I'll start carrying pepper spray during the day as well," I joked. "Mom, it's okay. I realize I put myself in a bad position, and I'll try not to do that again."

"Good." She walked over and gave me a quick hug. "Now, who do you think the murderer is? Because I'm not inclined to believe that boy Rusty did it. And I also don't think he's twenty-two. Did you check his ID?"

I held back an eye roll. "I think his ID might be fake, but that's not exactly where my priorities are right now. Underage drinking is going to have to take a back seat when there is a murderer here at the campground."

She nodded. "Agreed. So, who's your top suspect?"

I held up my hands. "Heck if I know. If Paul was the intended victim, then I can't see anyone besides Rusty being a suspect. But if Rusty was the intended victim…well, I've got even less to go on there. He seems like a nice guy. No one hates him. No one is accusing him of peeing on their tent or sleeping with their wife." I hesitated. "Well except for Charlie, but he seems to think everyone is sleeping with his wife. I thought I might have to kick the Masons out of the campground, but I never thought I might have to kick Charlie out."

Mom frowned. "Do you think he did it? If he thought Rusty was sleeping with Adelaide, then would he be jealous enough to try to kill him?"

I blew out a breath. "That seem so ridiculous, but people kill and hurt others for some really ridiculous reasons. Maybe? I don't know. Adelaide and Charlie were arguing outside the cabins this afternoon and Adelaide has some secret she's been keeping from her husband. For all I know, she did cheat on him. Even if seeing Adelaide exchanging a few words with Rusty was the last straw, I can't see him attempting to murder Rusty. The motive just seems…well, shaky."

"Well, the only way you knew about Paul peeing on that guy's tent was because he confessed to it while drunk. For all we know Rusty's been peeing on tents as well, or stealing stuff while people are out hiking. He seems nice, but we don't really know anything about him."

I shook my head. "I can't believe someone would attempt

to murder another over stolen camping equipment or minor vandalism."

"People kill other people in road rage incidents. People murder their estranged spouses and their new boyfriends. People shoot their supposed best friends over cheating at card games." Mom shrugged. "It could have been anyone, and for a reason that might sound ridiculous to us. If you're really thinking that one of the guests tampered with the food, then we probably should look at the security footage."

I did a double-take. "The what-what?"

"Security camera footage." Mom pointed into a corner of the store. "There's one outside as well, but I don't think that would do us much good. Best to start with this one and see what we can see."

I stared at her. "Since when do we have security cameras?"

"Since last week," Mom cheerfully announced.

It was a good idea—one I felt foolish for not thinking of myself. They were cheap enough and with money in the register as well as beer and wine in the fridge, having cameras was a smart precaution.

"They weren't expensive, and so easy to set up," Mom continued. "There's the one here in the camp store, one on the camp store porch that points out toward the fire pit, one by the garage where we keep the boats locked up, and one on the corner of the maintenance shed pointing to the camp store. I tried to balance the importance of guest privacy with our security needs, so outside of the one that overlooks the fire pit, all the others are focused on areas that I thought were most likely to see theft."

I looked at the small dome camera in the corner of the store and was amazed that I hadn't even noticed it.

"How did you install them?" I asked. Mom was pretty spry for eight-five, but she didn't like to be up on ladders.

"Austin helped. He mounted the cameras for me, and I installed the app and got them all up and running." She pulled out her phone and tapped on it before turning it to me. "See? I can swipe and see each camera in real-time as an individual picture, or have them displayed in mosaic. I can also view up to a year's worth of footage just by typing in the date."

"A *year*?" Had these things improved that much? I'd always thought they had limited storage and overwrote the footage every few days. Maybe that was just a plot device in cop shows, though.

"The cameras themselves only hold about forty-eight hours. The manufacturer recommends backing up to a hard drive every night, but I set them up to automatically synch with cloud storage in real-time. That way if someone smashes the camera or takes it, we still have the footage."

"That's...that's brilliant," I said, still trying to wrap my head around the fact that we had security cameras and that Mom had taken the initiative to do all of this. This was something *I* should have thought of, and I was so glad Mom had.

"I'm sorry I didn't tell you, honey," Mom said with an apologetic smile. "We've been so busy, and I forgot to mention it. And honestly, you have enough to worry about as it is. This campground is supposed to be a joyful undertaking. I know you love to be busy and that providing a wonderful vacation for the guests *is* a joyful activity as far as you are concerned. Still, I wish you'd take more time to enjoy the things you always loved about this campground when *you* were the guest here. I wish you'd let me help you more, so you could relax."

I was trying. I truly was. And in the course of relaxing on a lovely hike with Elvis, I'd found the body of one of our guests.

But I understood what Mom was saying. I needed to sit on the dock in the sun, enjoying the birdsong and the fresh breeze off the lake. I needed to take one of the canoes or kayaks out and paddle until my muscles burned, exploring the marshes and inlets—maybe even trying my hand at catching a fish. I needed to hike more, to see the sunset from an overlook, to watch the deer, the squirrels, the bear.

Okay, maybe not the bear—or maybe from a very far distance. I still wasn't sure about bear.

"Thank you for thinking about potential robberies and taking precautions," I told my mother. "I appreciate that you took the initiative on this and got it done. And please let me know if there are other things you want to do. I want *you* to have joyful experiences as well, and I don't want you to push yourself beyond what you can."

Mom sighed. "I'm well aware that if I don't speak up and insist that I take on chores, you'll just do it all yourself. That's who you've been your whole life, Sassy. Can't expect you to change at the age of fifty-eight now, can I? I'll speak up when I think you're taking on too much of your own and not letting me share the burden."

"Thank you." I clapped my hands and grinned. "Now, shall we watch some movies? Should I get the popcorn?"

CHAPTER 21

"There's Sierra bringing in the box of food," Mom narrated. "Goodness, that woman must be up at three A.M. to get all that baking done and be here at six with the delivery."

"I think she's discovered the secret to feeling rested with only four hours of sleep a night," I commented, passing the bowl of popcorn to my mother. Elvis begged me with his droopy hound eyes to share, so I tossed him a few of the buttery exploded kernels, hoping I wouldn't pay for my generosity later when the butter disagreed with Elvis's stomach.

We'd hung the "closed" sign on the camp store and gone back to the house to watch the camera footage on my laptop since the computer in the store was too ancient to handle the video, and squinting at Mom's phone wasn't optimal.

"Do you think I should let my hair grow out again?" I commented, watching myself on the footage.

My hair had never been much longer than shoulder-length, but I'd shaved it when clumps began to fall out from my chemo treatment. Even after it started to grow back, I'd kept it super short, allowing my hair time to fill in to a reasonable amount of thickness. Right now it was still in a short pixie cut, the silvery-gray locks slightly wavy. From my cancer survivor groups, I'd learned the waviness would go away, and that my hair would eventually return to the way it was before my diagnosis and treatment.

Other parts of my body would never return to the way they were before my diagnosis and treatment. I'd made my peace with that, and a part of me wanted to keep my hair short, as a sort of homage to survivorship. But looking at myself through the slightly distorted fish-eye of the camera lens, I wondered if the short hair was less feminine than the way I'd had it before.

Although why I was concerned about being "feminine" at this point in my life, I didn't know.

"I like it short," Mom announced. "It suits your face. And you've got a nice shaped head for that sort of hairdo. Plus, it's got to be easier to deal with. I know what a pain it was for you to style when it was long."

I nodded in agreement, remembering the mousse, the gel, the volumizing spray and the blow-dryer with the round brush. My hair was baby-fine and had looked limp and straggly without a whole lot of product and work. And that product and work had to be done every morning because, my hair needed to be washed every day. No amount of dry shampoo could overcome my greasy scalp.

I still needed to shampoo every day, but my current pixie cut dried in no time without a blow drier, and it required just a dollop of gel or a spritz of beach-spray to give it some lift. And if I didn't have time to wash it, a cute ballcap covered it all up.

"Oh, look! A customer!" Mom announced, distracting me from my weird thought-segue on hair styling choices.

"It's Jimmie Free from cabin eight," I told her, instantly

recognizing the man and his iconic hat. "He tries to get out on the lake before sunrise to fish. The man rented a canoe for every day of his stay, and he likes to be the first out there so he gets his favorite canoe."

All the canoes looked the same to me, but this guy had his favorite. I wasn't going to argue with him. If he wanted to haul himself out of bed at dark o'clock so he got his pick of the boats, then more power to him.

Mom and I ate popcorn and watched as Sierra left, and as guests came and went. Not all of them had food orders. A good many of the early risers were just grabbing bait, or coffee, or some trail mix and bottled drinks for their day. The ones that did have food orders seemed to quickly paw through the bags, grabbing theirs and either buying additional items or just heading out the door. I cameoed quite a bit, pointing different guests toward their food in the fridge or helping people find what they were searching for. At one point, I vanished into the back room, leaving two guests in the store unattended.

"Stop," I said, sitting up in my chair. "Back that one up about thirty seconds."

Mom complied and I watched as Charlie and Lexi came through the door and moved about the store.

"He wanted to know if we had any more of the bottles of chocolate milk in the back," I remembered. "Lexi liked them and we didn't have any in the store fridge."

"We didn't have any because he bought six the night before," Mom commented. "Good grief. How much chocolate milk does that girl drink?"

"Maybe he's drinking it himself and blaming Lexi because it's not cool for a grown man to be drinking six bottles of chocolate milk in one night," I commented, watching the video. "Slow it down to half speed. There. I'm heading into the back room. Charlie and Lexi are over at the food box, going through the bags."

"Did he order food?" Mom asked, frowning.

"Yes, he did. For both himself and Lexi."

"He's taking a long time over that food box," Mom commented. "You'd think it wouldn't be so hard to find two bags with his and his daughter's names. Did his wife have an order as well?"

"No." That had bothered me. Why order a sandwich for yourself and your daughter, but not your wife? He hadn't even called her to ask if she wanted something, or come back later to add hers to his order. Was he a controlling jerk in addition to being a jealous jerk?

"There." I pointed my finger at the screen and Mom paused the footage. "It's hard to see from the angle, but it looks like he took a bag out, pulled something from the bag, and unwrapped it. Then he wraps it back up, returns it to the bag, and puts it back into the box."

Mom and I stared at the frozen screen for a few seconds.

"I'm going to play devil's advocate here," Mom slowly said. "Maybe Sierra's handwriting is a little off and there's another guest named Charlie or something close to it. He takes the bag out, goes to check the sandwich to make sure the order is correct—because lots of people do that, Sassy—then he realizes it's not his order and puts it back."

That was absolutely believable, but so was an alternate explanation. "Or he sees Rusty's order, and quickly pulls it out and puts something in the sandwich while I'm in the back looking for chocolate milk—chocolate milk *he* bought all of the night before"

"Maybe." Mom's voice was full of doubt. "Let's watch the rest of the tape and see if there's anything else—anything that shows someone *clearly* putting something on a sandwich and returning it to the box."

We continued to watch. I returned from the back storeroom with the chocolate milk. Charlie paid for Lexi's purchases and left with the food order bags in his hand. Others came and went, but no one lingered over the box, or returned any of the bags after checking the sandwiches inside. Lots of people unwrapped their sandwiches, but were clearly satisfied that their order was correct. Nothing appeared untoward, but watching the tape made me realize we'd made the right decision to keep the food behind the counter in the future. I liked that we were in a small rural town and ran a homey, country campground, but with our camping season about ready to head into no-vacancy mode, we couldn't take the chance that someone would grab the wrong order or tamper with someone else's food. Eventually Rusty came in, heading straight for the box and pulling out the bags for himself and his brothers.

Rusty left after getting the food and I paused the replay.

"Well, that was ambiguous," I announced. "I don't know what I was hoping for. Maybe someone standing in clear view of the camera and tampering with the sandwich after holding the bag up so we could read the name on it first?"

"That would have been very convenient," Mom agreed. "But real life is rarely convenient."

I nodded. "So I'm going to say right now it wasn't Sierra. I know Jake has to look into her as a suspect, but I don't. She's my friend, and I'm positive she wouldn't have killed Paul, or even *wanted* to kill Rusty. She just wanted the Masons to leave and not come back. Unless there was a reoccurrence of what happened last year, Sierra would have kept to a few verbal confrontations. She wouldn't want to chance the embarrassment and exposure that a murder investigation would bring. She just wanted it all to go away."

"I agree," Mom said. "But can we rule out an employee of Sierra's? Someone who might have tampered with the sandwich while the box was left unattended in the van? Someone who might want to do *her* harm through having her accused of murder?"

"I'd thought about that too, but I just can't see someone having an opportunity." I frowned in thought. "Sierra brings the box of food in right after she parks, and she comes straight from the shop with the order, so I don't see there being a chance for someone to tamper with the sandwich while it was in the van. Likewise, I can't imagine Flora doing this, especially since it was Paul she and Sierra were upset with, not Rusty."

"Maybe there's a campground guest who was jilted by Rusty and is stalking him, so she knew he was planning a vacation. She followed him here, disguised herself and tried to remain unnoticed while she waited for her opportunity to poison him." Mom shrugged at my laugh. "Or maybe not."

"Okay, now we are seriously going down a rabbit hole here." I looked at the laptop screen once more. "Either Rusty put something in the sandwich, knowing that he was going to give it to Paul to eat, or Peter put something in the sandwich because he wanted to kill Rusty, or one of the guests wants Rusty dead."

Our heads both swiveled to the screen in synchronized motion.

"It has to be Charlie." Mom rewound the footage on the laptop and hit play again.

I growled in frustration as we watched the tape. "I can't really see what he's doing because he's partially got his back to the camera. He could have just been checking the sandwiches or misreading the name on the bag, but he's now my top suspect. And I don't know why other than I don't like him."

"You said he accused Rusty of sleeping with Adelaide?" Mom asked.

I nodded. "Yes, but both she and Rusty swear they both just spoke casually. Is there something going on I don't know about? Did Charlie catch Rusty coming out of their RV or something?"

Mom sniffed. "If he caught another man coming out of the RV, we would have had a second, more violent brawl on the campground property."

"You're right." I ran a hand through my hair. "So if it's Charlie, is he just angry at all attractive men who speak to his wife and look like they're barely out of their teens? I mean, there are other good-looking men here closer to Adelaide's age. Why would he target Rusty in this way?"

Mom paused the footage right where Charlie was unwrapping a sandwich. "You said the woman had secrets. Maybe Rusty is one of her secrets. If she was sleeping around, she'd be careful not to appear at all interested in the man with her husband or anyone else nearby. And some women like younger men, just as some men like younger women. Maybe there is a vacation fling going on—one that has been carefully hidden. Not that a fling gives Charlie the right to murder someone, but he might have more motive than you think."

I stared at the screen, doubting my ability to read and judge people's morals once more. Was Rusty secretly a killer? An adulterer? Was tearful Adelaide actually sleeping around on her husband and gaslighting him?

I'd bought this campground envisioning years of fun planned activities, happy and restful guests, and me soaking up the sunshine and enjoying life surrounded by nature. Instead here I was facing a second death in less than a month —a second murder.

I wasn't going to let this define my business. I'd keep my word to Jake about not taking unnecessary risks, but I was still going to poke my nose into this investigation and do what I could to find out who murdered one of my guests.

And yes, I did realize that my promise to him had lasted less than two hours.

I hit the play button on the laptop and watched once more as Charlie took the bag from the box, opened it and the sandwich, then blocked everything from the camera view. The only person who knew what he'd done was Charlie himself.

And a little girl who was clearly watching everything her father did, her fingers slowly lifting toward her mouth as her brows furrowed.

CHAPTER 22

"Is there a way you can send this footage to Jake?" I asked Mom. "All of it. Not just the one from the camp store, but the last three days of footage from all cameras. Let him know that yesterday's tape from the camp store might be the most relevant, but there could be something else he could pick up from the other footage that we didn't have time to look at."

Not that Jake probably had the time to look at them either. I felt a bit guilty sending him days of video from four different cameras. Even fast-forwarding and skimming, it would take him at least a full day to review all of this. Still, I wanted local law enforcement to have everything they needed to catch the killer.

While Mom was doing that, I rooted through the boxes of craft supplies that I'd gotten from the attic and hauled them over to the camp store where I had additional boxes of craft supplies. Selecting a dozen or so items, I pulled a canvas bag from another box and wrote "Lexi" on it with one of the few glitter pens I'd found that hadn't completely dried up.

Then I went down the road toward the cabins, waving as

I passed a few of our guests who were sitting out on lawn chairs, enjoying the spring sunshine.

There was no sign of Adelaide, but Lexi was sitting on a stool next to Denver Twigg, her short legs dangling as she painted. The girl had a nonstop commentary going on that I could hear from three cabins away. To his credit, Denver didn't seem at all bothered by the interruption in his creative process. He'd occasionally grunt in acknowledgement, but otherwise he appeared to be ignoring the young girl as he focused on his own artwork.

As I approached, I realized that he wasn't ignoring her at all. He was painting her. The abstract of red and turquoise trees with a gray and muted blue backdrop of a choppy lake featured a young girl walking down a path. Her features were indistinct, her form little more than bold brushstrokes of dark crimson, but the lively posture suggested a triumph over adversity, a forward momentum in the face of tragedy.

I blinked back tears once more, amazed at how sentimental I'd gotten over the last two years.

"How are our resident artists doing?" I asked, a bit self-conscious about interrupting the man who was clearly creating some serious art.

"I like painting," Lexi announced. "I want to be an artist when I grow up."

"You don't need to wait until you grow up to be an artist," Denver said in a gruff voice. "Artists create whether they're two or two hundred."

"No one is two hundred," Lexi countered. "That's just silly. People don't live past thirty."

I coughed to cover a laugh at that, and saw Denver's lips twitch.

"I like your painting," I said as I leaned over the girl's shoulder to see her canvas. I was no art critic, but it looked pretty darned good to me. She'd clearly tried to emulate

Denver's style, but had given it her own flair with a cacophony of primary colors and a pack of dogs scattered between trees, and a rudimentary cabin beside a lake, smoke pouring from the chimney.

"That's Elvis," she said, pointing at one of the dogs whose ears were a good bit longer than the other ones on the painting.

"An excellent likeness," I told her. "Is that a boat out on the lake?"

She nodded. "It's the canoe Daddy and I took out fishing yesterday afternoon. He didn't catch anything, so he was grumpy. I didn't catch anything either, but that didn't make me grumpy. I like the boat and the water and looking at the fish and animals. It was fun."

"I'm sorry your father was grumpy," I said, treading carefully and trying to plan how to approach the questions I wanted to ask.

"He's grumpy a lot." She sighed. "I know he's mad at Mommy, but he won't tell me why and Mommy just looks upset when I ask her."

I felt my heart twist at that.

"Is your mom in the cabin?" I asked, thinking it would be best if I asked Adelaide before taking Lexi over to the camp store.

The girl shook her head. "She went back to the RV to get some of our things. She said she might go for a walk to think a bit and that I should stay here and paint with Dorito Man."

Dorito Man. I choked back another laugh at the fact that she'd saddled my guest with the moniker.

"I don't know why Daddy's angry at *me*," she continued. "I kept his secret. I didn't tell anyone. And I wanted to stay in the camper instead of sharing a bed with Mommy in a cabin."

I glanced over at Denver, thinking I should take this conversation into a more private area.

"I've got some painting supplies that I put together into bag for you to take home with you," I told Lexi. "Would you like to come over to the camp store with me to get it? I'll bring you right back here and Mr. Twigg can tell your mother where you are if she comes looking for you."

She hesitated a moment, looking over at the cabin, then off in the direction of the camper, then to "Dorito Man."

"Okay. As long as Mommy knows where I am, it's okay."

"I'll tell her if she comes by before you're back," Denver said. "And you can trust Miss Sassy to keep you safe. She's a nice lady."

Lexi slipped off her stool and slid her hand into mine. "She is nice."

My heart warmed at that. I led her back down the gravel drive toward the camp store. When we got within sight of the porch, she waved at Elvis who was sprawled at the top of the steps, his long tail wagging as he watched us.

I unhooked the hound as we climbed the steps and we all went inside once I unlocked the door to the camp store.

"Here it is." I went behind the counter then came out and handed Lexi the bag with her name written on the front. Her mouth made an "o" and she set it on the floor, going through the supplies.

"Thank you, Miss Sassy! Thank you!" She squealed as she pulled out a fist-full of brushes. "These are just like the ones Dorito Man has!"

I was pretty sure those ten-for-a-dollar brushes were not the same ones a professional artist had, but I didn't correct her.

"I'm glad you like it. Now you can paint at home as well," I told her. "There are paints as well as some small canvases in there and a pack of watercolor papers too."

"I like painting," she announced as she returned the items to the bag. "But I liked the craft project with the nuts and twigs as well. Maybe I'll do some multi-media art. That's what Dorito Man said it was called."

"That would be lovely. But I think the picture you did this morning, was very nice. I especially like your including Elvis in your painting," I said.

"You can have it," she told me. "As long as you hang it in the camp store and put my name under it on a plaque. That's what Dorito Man says happens in art displays and galleries."

I bit back a smile. "I would love to display your art here, and will definitely post a plaque under it with your name as well as the title of the piece. You know we're keeping the food deliveries behind the counter now, so everyone will see it."

My subtle segue didn't seem to register because the girl just nodded and continued to look through the bag of art supplies.

"We put the box of sandwiches behind the counter because we were worried that someone might accidently pick up the wrong one," I added.

Her head shot up at that and her expression registered a wary uneasiness. "Sometimes the names look the same. It's easy to get the wrong sandwich," she said.

I nodded and decided to take a chance here. "Like your dad. He accidently picked up the wrong sandwich yesterday, but he realized it and put it back so he could get the right one."

Relief blossomed over the girl's face. "It wasn't his fault. He put it back. He'd accidently put his special spice on it first, so he told me to not tell anyone. People are funny about others touching their food, and the person whose sandwich it was might not like his special spice. He didn't want to ruin that man's lunch, so it was our secret. Did the other man complain? Daddy can pay for his sandwich if he did. It was a mistake."

I caught my breath, my mind whirling at the thought that I'd caught a killer. I just wasn't positive why Charlie had done it, and I wasn't sure there was enough evidence to convict him. Maybe he'd just sprinkled Old Bay seasoning on a different sandwich? I could be going down the wrong path here. I wasn't a trained investigator and I might be getting this all wrong.

But then I remembered the order form I'd looked at when Jake had been here. Charlie had ordered ham and Swiss on whole wheat toast with lettuce, tomato, and black pepper. He would have known the moment he'd unwrapped Rusty's grilled veggie on lettuce that it wasn't his. Why would he have put his "special spice" on a sandwich that clearly wasn't his?

"What's your daddy's special spice?" I smiled at Lexi. "I like a few shakes of Tabasco myself, but a friend of mine always put A.1. Steak Sauce on her sandwiches."

She shrugged, still looking at the markers and stickers and other items I'd put in her gift bag. "I don't know. I've never seen him put anything on his food at home, but he said it was his special spice. It was a white powder, but some of it was kinda chunky like it wasn't ground up enough. He sprinkled it out of a brown plastic bottle. Maybe it was salt. My aunt puts salt on everything and likes the pink stuff in a grinder. She carries it in her purse and puts it on food at restaurants. Mom says that's weird, but I don't see anything wrong with putting special spices on foods. I like ranch dressing. When I grow up, I'm going to carry ranch dressing in my purse and put it on all *my* sandwiches."

"Do you remember the name on the bag?" I asked, trying not to laugh at the vision of a grown-up Lexi pulling a bottle of ranch dressing out of her purse. "The one that your dad got by mistake?"

She scrunched up her brows then shook her head. "No. I wasn't really paying attention."

"Do you remember what the sandwich looked like?" I pressed.

She thought for a moment. "It was gross. A bunch of veggies with brown sauce wrapped up in lettuce. Daddy says if people want sandwiches they need to eat them on bread like God intended."

I held back a laugh, because I also liked bread, although I wouldn't turn down a lettuce wrap either.

"Does your dad ever eat that kind of food?" I asked. "Veggies with brown sauce wrapped in lettuce?"

"No." She shook her head. "He put his special spice on real quick and didn't realize until after that he'd made a mistake, so he wrapped it up and put it back and told me not to tell anyone. Did that person complain?"

I thought of Paul Mason, dead in the morgue. "No, he didn't complain."

"Good." She sighed. "Daddy didn't want to get in trouble. I didn't want him to get in trouble either. Sometimes people make mistakes."

"Yes, they do," I said, thinking that this felt more than just a mistake. But why? Had Charlie been driven to this after weeks or months of stewing, thinking his wife was cheating on him? Were Adelaide and Rusty really having a vacation fling as Mom had suggested?

I helped Lexi gather her art supplies into the bag I'd written her name on, and walked her back to the cabin she and her mother had moved into. Denver was still painting, Lexi's easel and canvas and stool still beside him.

"Finish your painting," I told the girl as we walked over to her stool. "And when your mom comes back, let her know that I'd like to talk to her when she's got a moment."

I left the girl and the man happily painting and walked

back. The short walk to the store I was deep in thought. Should I text Jake with my suspicions, letting him know what Lexi had revealed? Should I wait until I spoke with Adelaide first? Should I just butt out of the whole thing and let the police deal with it?

As I walked back to the camp store, I made a decision—I pulled my phone out of my pocket and texted Jake.

CHAPTER 23

*J*ake stood before me, disheveled and annoyed. He hadn't left here more than three hours ago. I assumed when I texted him he'd been watching the footage Mom sent over, but he looked like he'd been crawling through bushes, not looking at grainy images on his computer.

"You *promised* me you wouldn't confront anyone," he scolded.

I reached out to pick a bit of hay off his shirt. "I questioned a six-year-old girl. That's hardly confronting someone, and the six-year-old girl isn't the murderer."

"No, but she might have told her father about your conversation, and *he's* most likely the murderer," Jake pointed out. "And he's right here, at your campground, where he could be at the camp store bludgeoning you to death in a whole lot less time than it would take me to drive down the mountain."

He had a point.

"I texted you right away," I pointed out. "And I left Lexi happily painting with Denver Twigg, not running to tell her father. There was time for you to drive down the mountain before any bludgeoning got started."

"I'm still not happy." He scowled.

"I see that." I let him stew in his unhappiness for a few seconds. "Can we now move on to the murderer? I don't know if you've watched all the footage from inside the camp store or not."

"I have," he snapped, obviously not moving on.

"Charlie was the only one who lingered over the selections. I remember when I came out of the storeroom with the chocolate milk, he had a bunch of bags out of the box on the table. I didn't see what the name on those bags were, but he quickly put them all back. When I asked his daughter, she said he 'accidentally' opened a grilled veggie wrapped in lettuce and put his 'special spice' on it before he allegedly realized it was the wrong sandwich and put it all back. Rusty's was the only grilled veggie wrap on lettuce that day. All the other ones had the flour wraps. He put ground up pills on Rusty's sandwich. I don't know if you had the labs analyze the food by the body—"

"We did, as well as the contents of his water bottle, the coffee, the chips, and the apple core," Jake said, his tone a bit warmer.

"Was it the opiates they found in his system? Oh, I'll bet you can't tell me that, can you?"

"You can always ask Lottie," he quipped. "I'm sure she knows."

I laughed. "True. If it was the sandwich though, then the killer *has* to be Charlie. I don't know if Rusty and Adelaide are actually having an affair or not, but Charlie clearly thinks they are."

"Sean is busy digging into Charlie's background," Jake told me. "Oliver is getting a warrant to search the camper and to access his electronic records."

I frowned. "You're searching the camper for the rest of the pills? He might not have any more. Or he might have tossed them and the container after he put them on the sandwich."

"Or he could have kept some in case Rusty didn't eat the sandwich," Jake pointed out. "And there are other things we're looking for as well. Things that might also establish motive, planning, and intent."

"Like proof of the affair," I mused. "Notes, texts, e-mails, phone calls."

"Exactly." Jake looked around the camp store. "We're going to go to the cabin to see Adelaide and ask her to come here to the camp store where it's private so we can talk. She'll most likely think you told the police about the argument this morning and that you're going to try to convince her to file for a peace order. It's not typical procedure, but I'd also like you to hang around while I question her. You've made a connection with her and I think she might be more open to talking with you present."

I nodded, torn between excitement and sadness. Poor Adelaide. She loved her husband, and it was so unfair that this was happening to her. And Lexi. My heart hurt for the little girl.

"Okay," I said.

"I want the little girl to stay with that other man, painting," Jake continued. "You said that Adelaide had gone to get stuff from the camper. That worries me. If she's not back and at the cabin when we go to bring her here, I'll call Sean for backup and I'll go to the camper for a welfare check. If that happens, you need to get the little girl and go somewhere safe. Understand?"

Suddenly the serious nature of it all hit me and I was no longer excited. "Yes, I understand."

"When she gets here, I want you to let me take the lead on

the questions. You offered her that cabin because you were concerned about possible domestic violence, so she'll assume that's why I'm here. She'll most likely defend her husband, but I'm hoping once I lay out the evidence that he may have attempted to murder Rusty Mason, she'll talk."

I nodded, then got my leash and took Elvis with us as we walked toward the cabins. Jake was far more protection than my hound, but I hoped that Elvis would reduce the inevitable tension of us asking Adelaide to come to the camp store to "talk." As we walked, I glanced over at Jake, and noted that although he still didn't have any sort of uniform, he had a badge clipped to his belt along with all sorts of other things —including a holster with a pistol.

I'd never seen him with a pistol before. His loose but agile gait, the firearm at his hip, the stony set of his expression all made me nervous. I wiped my hands on my pants, and looked at Elvis who was oblivious to the tension. The hound bounced as he walked by my side, his long tail high and wagging, his mouth open in a happy-pant. He wasn't worried, but Jake was, and I wasn't sure who to take my cue from.

"Relax," Jake muttered. "You look like you're heading up the gallows steps."

"I can't help but be tense," I muttered back. "You look like you're ten paces away from shooting someone."

He didn't reply. I tried to take his advice and relax, waving at Lexi and Denver, and shaking my hands out to relieve the tension in them as I climbed the porch steps to the cabin.

To my relief, Adelaide answered on the first knock. She smiled at me, the smile fading as she saw Jake, then completely vanishing as her gaze landed on the badge.

"This isn't necessary," she whispered, glancing over at

Lexi. "Everything is okay. I don't need the police to get involved."

"Can we talk about this at the camp store?" I asked her. "Away from prying eyes and Lexi? He just wants to go over some options with you. After what happened this morning, I thought it would be a good idea."

"There's no pressure, ma'am," Jake said, his smooth Georgia accent kicking in. "I just want to make sure you're okay and that you know of all the resources we have available here in Reckless. Besides, my momma would kill me if I didn't do all I could to help a woman in need."

His momma? I barely restrained myself from registering surprise at that. He'd never mentioned his parents, and I'd just assumed they had passed. Did he have a mother, and possibly a father, alive in Georgia? Brothers and sisters? The idea intrigued me and I found myself wanting to know a whole lot more about Jake Bailey.

"Fine." Adelaide's mouth was set in a thin line. "Let me lock up and we'll go to the camp store. Lexi," she called out, "you stay here with Mr. Twigg. Mommy will be right back."

It was a quiet walk back to the camp store. Once inside, I unhooked Elvis's leash to let him roam and went to pour us all some coffee. Jake motioned for Adelaide to sit at the little café table and pulled another chair over before sitting across from her. I brought over the coffee, sugar, and creamer. Elvis, clearly sensing that all was not well, walked over to Adelaide and put his head on her lap.

"Several people at the campground have been concerned about your husband's interactions with you," Jake started. "Has he ever put his hands on you in anger? Or on Lexi?"

"No!" Adelaide sat back in her chair. "Like I told Sassy, since his mother died, he's been emotional. And with me returning to work…he's been quick to anger. He keeps thinking I'm having an affair. But he's never touched me or Lexi in anger. Never."

"Were you having an affair?" Jake slid the question in there as if he were inquiring about the weather.

"No! I'd never do that. I love my husband. From the moment we became engaged I haven't even looked at another man," she protested.

"But there has to be a reason he suspects you're having an affair," I said, forgetting about Jake's instructions to keep silent. "He accused you of having secrets. Was there someone? Maybe you didn't sleep with him, but you had an e-mail romance? Texted?"

Her eyes flashed. "I thought this was about me getting resources in leaving my husband, not an interrogation about whether I've had an affair or not. But to answer your question, no. I've never had an e-mail romance or anything. Yes, I have secrets, but they're not my secrets to tell. I'm not going to ruin other people's lives by revealing things that happened twenty years ago."

Twenty years ago. Something niggled at the back of my brain about that.

"Can you tell me when you first met Rusty Mason?" Jake asked her, ignoring my interruption.

She stiffened. "When we came to the campground. We ran into each other Thursday night and exchanged pleasantries. I didn't speak to him again until Saturday afternoon. I'd heard about his brother having a heart attack on the trail and dying, so I offered my condolences. Charlie saw us talking on Saturday and misread the situation. The last month or two he's been suspicious of every man I've spoken to."

Jake nodded. "So Charlie didn't see you talking to Rusty on Thursday night?"

Adelaide hesitated. "I…I don't think so. Why? What has any of this to do with my marital issues?"

Jake's gaze fixed on Adelaide. "Paul Mason didn't die of a heart attack. Someone murdered him. And he wasn't the intended victim. We believe Rusty Mason was."

Adelaide's face blanched. Her hands shook and her mouth trembled.

"So, of course, we're exploring who might have wanted to kill Rusty Mason. Your jealous husband accused you of sleeping with him," Jake continued.

"He wouldn't…" Her voice broke. "Oh, God. Charlie…no. It can't be true. He'd never do that."

"We have surveillance footage from inside the camp store of him tampering with a sandwich that was in a bag with Rusty's name on it," Jake told her. "Your daughter witnessed it. She said Charlie called it his 'special spice' and that it was all just a mistake in getting the wrong sandwich. But your husband had ordered something completely different from Rusty's sandwich."

Adelaide put her hands over her face. "No. Just…no."

"Paul accidentally left his sandwich behind on their hike, so Rusty gave his to his brother," Jake continued. "Paul died of an opiate overdose, and we found crushed oxycodone on the remains of the sandwich he was eating—Rusty's sandwich."

Adelaide began to sob.

"Your husband tried to kill Rusty Mason, and caused Paul Mason's death." Jake's voice became firm and authoritative. "Your husband tried to kill your lover."

"He's not my lover," Adelaide cried out. "He's my brother."

CHAPTER 24

*S*he dissolved into sobs. Jake and I exchanged a quick surprised glance and I got up to grab a box of tissues while Elvis nudged the distraught woman with his nose.

I handed her the box of tissues, and Jake and I waited until she'd managed to get control of her emotions enough to speak again.

"A year ago, I decided to start tracing my family's ancestry," Adelaide said, her voice still choked. "Lexi was in preschool and I thought it would be fun to look into my family tree. I even sent away a DNA sample. Then I got one of those alerts that said they'd matched my DNA to people on the site. Most of them were cousins, but there was a match to a man named Philip Mason. I thought it must be some sort of accident, but he contacted me because he'd gotten the notice of the match as well. We e-mailed back and forth a bit and found out that my dad and his mom had worked for the same company twenty years ago. He said his mom had quit the job when she was pregnant with him, then soon after his parents had divorced. He'd been curious because his DNA match with his two brothers hadn't been as strong as it should have been. His mother had died when he was fifteen, but after we'd e-mailed, he went through some of her letters and journals and found out that she'd had an affair with an unnamed man at her job. Philip, who goes by Rusty, believed that man had been his father, and that the affair had spelled the end of his parents' marriage."

Tears spilled down Adelaide's face, and I pushed the tissue box closer to her. She pulled one out and blew her nose before continuing.

"Rusty and I had the DNA test redone, because I just couldn't believe my father would do such a thing. There had been no hint of trouble in my parent's marriage, and I would have been about Lexi's age at the time. My mother was oblivious. I asked her a few discrete questions, and it was clear she'd never known. The second DNA results were the same. In fact, they had even more detail since I'd paid to have a private lab run the test. Rusty and I were half siblings. My father had cheated on my mother, and his mother had become pregnant."

I felt this right in my gut. I'd been cheated on and had been completely oblivious as well. The only difference was that my husband had left me for the other woman, and they'd never had children together. Still, the pain of betrayal, the embarrassing burn of being the fool, raced through me even though my husband's affair had occurred decades ago.

Some things could never be forgiven, no matter how long ago they had occurred.

"I don't know if my dad knows about Rusty or not." Adelaide wiped her eyes. "It was all in the past, and I knew that if it came out, it would ruin my parents' marriage. I didn't want to cause my mother that pain. And Rusty felt the same way. He didn't want his mother's memory to be smirched, or his brothers to regard him as any less than a full sibling. We decided it was best to let it all remain a secret. But we were brother and sister, and neither one of us could keep from e-mailing each other and keeping in touch."

"Charlie found out," I surmised.

She held up her hands. "I guess he did. I deleted the e-mails, but he must have found something. After his mother died, he became possessive, smothering. When I went back to work it got worse. I didn't connect any of it until I arrived at the campground and saw Rusty. At first I thought it was just a weird coincidence, that Charlie had accidently booked our vacation at the same time and place as Rusty and his brothers. Savage Lake is a popular vacation spot, and both Charlie and I had been getting advertisements in our Facebook feeds for the campground as well as on the app we downloaded when we bought the camper."

"I *have* been advertising a lot," I told Jake.

"Rusty and I agreed to just act like we didn't know each other, to avoid each other. We didn't speak again until after his brother died. I felt like I had to say something to him, to tell him how sorry I was. He's my brother, and I know how much he was hurting over losing someone he loved. Charlie saw us that night and confronted me. We argued all last night, and this morning I took Sassy up on her offer to stay with Lexi in one of the cabins."

"Oh, Adelaide. I'm so sorry." I put a hand on the woman's shoulder.

"Does your husband have access to oxycodone or prescription strength pain killers?" Jake asked, seemingly unmoved by the tragedy.

She thought for a second, then nodded. "I don't recall him taking anything himself, but his mother died of cancer. She was on a whole bunch of medications. He went through the house after she passed, so he might have taken her meds. I know in the beginning she was on pills, then toward the end she was on a patch and some liquid painkiller that was so strong it had to be doled out by the hospice nurse. But I'm sure there were pills left from earlier that she'd gotten from the pharmacy. And they were probably high dose because the cancer had quickly spread to her spine and her bones and she'd been in a lot of pain."

Jake set down his notepad and pen. "Why didn't you tell your husband about your half-brother? That seems like the kind of thing that married people would share with each other."

Adelaide laughed, and the sound ended on a sob. "Charlie can't keep a secret to save his life. And he's triggered by infidelity. His father and his mother broke up because of an affair, and even though he works for his father's chain of car dealerships, he's never forgiven him for that. He was always closer to his mother. If I had told him about Rusty, he would have confronted my father and absolutely told my mother. I know he would never have been able to keep secret about it. I didn't want to ruin my parents' marriage, or to cause Rusty any grief, so I figured this little secret wouldn't matter."

"And when it was clear that Charlie suspected something between you and Rusty?" I asked. "When you had to choose between your husband and the secret affair your father had twenty years ago, you picked your cheating father?"

Her face reddened. "I picked my mother, and her love for my father. I didn't want to see her hurt. And Charlie's jealousy had started way before I'd even found out about Rusty. He's always been possessive, and it got worse after his mother died. Me telling him about Rusty wouldn't have changed anything. He would have been just as crazy if I'd been on a project with a male co-worker, or Lexi had a playdate with a kid who has a stay-at-home dad. Charlie needs help. And my ruining my parents' marriage and Rusty's family wouldn't change that."

Jake's phone beeped and he gave it a quick glance. "The sheriff is here with a warrant to search your camper. Will you unlock the door for us?"

Adelaide nodded and rose, her head lowered and shoulders slumped. "Yes. Can someone make sure Lexi doesn't see? I don't want her to know any of this is going on."

Jake looked at me and I stood as well. "I'll find something interesting that we both can do." *And I'll keep her somewhere safe.*

Jake and Adelaide headed toward the camper hookups, while I took Elvis and went back down the path toward the cabins. Lexi and I could walk in the woods, or play fetch with Elvis, or she could help me go through the craft supplies in the owner's house that I'd brought down from the attic. Whatever we did, I was determined that the girl would never see police searching their camper, or arresting her father.

CHAPTER 25

I hung the closed sign on the camp store door while Mom, Elvis, and I entertained Lexi in the house. Jake's warnings had finally sunk into my thick skin and I was afraid—afraid that Charlie would snap and decide to go out in a wild-west-style shootout with the cops. Would Jake die? Would Charlie survive and come to the owner's house to kill Mom and me and claim his daughter after slaughtering all the law enforcement of Reckless, his wife, and most of the campground guests?

It was hard to keep a cheerful front for Lexi while I whispered the details of what had happened to Mom all while longing to open up a bottle of booze and start drinking.

We played, fed Lexi dinner, watched videos on the laptop. The girl never once questioned why she'd been here so long or where her parents were. In fact, Lexi seemed perfectly happy doing crafts, playing with Elvis, and chatting with Mom and me.

At seven o'clock, I was startled by a knock at the door. Mom was hustling Lexi into the back bedroom and I'd grabbed the broom handle when Jake called out that it was him.

I opened the door.

He took one look at the broom handle in my hands and his eyebrows shot up. "Don't hit me. I come in peace."

"Very funny." I set the broom handle aside and motioned for him to come in. "What happened?"

He glanced at Mom and Lexi. "Let's go for a walk. Lexi, your mom will be here soon to take you home. I hope you had a good time with Miss Sassy and Miss Ellie Mae."

"I did have a good time," the girl piped up. "And with Elvis too. I love Elvis. Maybe Daddy will let me get a dog of my own."

I was probably the only one that saw Jake's wince.

Motioning for Elvis to stay in the house, I went out onto the porch then walked beside Jake down the steps and toward the camp store.

"We found the oxycodone pills in Charlie's shaving kit," Jake told me as we strolled. "He was blustering and arguing outside while we searched. When we confronted him with all the evidence, he confessed. And like the asshole he is, he blamed it all on Adelaide for supposedly sleeping around."

"Poor Adelaide." I glanced back at the house. "And poor Lexi."

Jake shook his head. "Adelaide was tearful, trying to convince him of her innocence until the very end. She never told him that Rusty was her brother."

"Even now, she chose her parents' marriage over her husband," I mused.

"She probably made the right choice. I think her husband was beyond saving. She might blame it all on his grief, but the guy's got issues. Even if he hadn't tried to kill Rusty and caused Paul's death, it would have just been a matter of time before he snapped." Jake blew out an exasperated breath. "Not that I agree with what Adelaide did. If her father had an affair and fathered a child, then his marriage is built on a lie, and Adelaide keeping that secret isn't doing either of her parents any favors. Plus I don't like that she kept this from Charlie. Married people need to be able to trust and confide in each other. My ex and I had an amicable divorce, but if I'd found sketchy stuff and suspected she was keeping things from me, I don't know if I could have ever trusted her again."

"I agree." I took a deep breath and let it out. "My ex cheated on me and I never knew it until he asked for a divorce. I trusted him, and it's been hard for me to trust anyone since then."

Jake shot me a sympathetic glance. "But you didn't go killing any of his supposed lovers."

I barked out a laugh. "No, I didn't. But I did eat a whole lot of ice cream. And I won't deny that the divorce was hard. It was a long time ago, the hurt still lingers."

There, that was as close to a confession of my emotions as I'd ever come with any of the men I'd known post-Richard.

"We arrested him." Jake sighed. "After arraignment they'll transfer him to Derwood or maybe Roanoke where they have long-term facilities pending trial. All we've got in Reckless is a two-cell jail mostly for holding drunks overnight. Although depending on the judge and his finances, he might post bail."

"His dad owns a bunch of car dealerships, so I think the family has money," I commented. "What will happen to Adelaide and Lexi? This has got to be so devastating for them. He didn't just ruin Paul Mason's and his own life, but his wife and daughter's as well."

Jake shrugged. "I don't know. She mentioned staying with a sister for a while. I think she plans on spending the night in the cabin, then leaving for home with Lexi tomorrow morning."

"With the camper?" I frowned, remembering how Charlie had struggled to drive the huge thing.

"She mentioned paying someone to tow it home for her. I don't blame her for not wanting to drive it. It's huge."

We came to a stop by his truck. "Thank you for coming by and letting me know what happened. Thank you for...everything."

He put his hands on my shoulders and turned me to face him. "Sassy, this has nothing to do with you or your campground. All my years as a cop have taught me that these things happen. People can be horrible, and where they choose to do their horrible stuff is all about them and not about the place where the crime happens. You couldn't have prevented any of this."

"Reckless hasn't had murders in ages, yet I show up and there are two in a month," I protested.

"The first technically happened before you got here." His lips quirked up in a smile. "You're not a crime magnet. So stop that train of thought right now. Even small towns have murders, and sometimes two happen in a month."

He was right. I wasn't some harbinger of doom. The important thing was that two killers had been caught and were now behind bars.

Argue as I may, Jake walked me back to the house then retraced our steps to the camp store. I watched his truck go down the lane. Then I watched as a fancy BMW sedan came up the lane, pulling to a stop in front of my house. Lottie jumped out. I noted her lilac pants and yellow and pink sweater set as she raced for my door.

I opened the door before she had a chance to knock.

"What did I miss?" she asked breathlessly pushing past me into the house. "I've been up on the widow's walk, watching all the police activity through my rifle scope. Was it that Rusty? Or Peter? Or someone else? Who'd they arrest?"

I closed the door, and motioned for her to sit. "I'll get us some coffee. We've got a lot of catching up to do."

"Coffee?" Lottie snorted, heading for the kitchen. "Girl, I think this calls for wine."

CHAPTER 26

I watched Adelaide and Lexi leave, feeling a bit bereft. The bright sunshine seemed to dim a bit as they drove down the drive, the young girl waving as she leaned out the side window of the truck.

Did she know? From the bright smile on her face, I was guessing her mother hadn't told her. It figured. Adelaide was good at keeping secrets. Although this was one secret she'd eventually have to reveal. Lexi was bound to wonder why her father wasn't coming home. As she got older, she'd find out on her own even if her mother never told her what had happened.

I doubted Adelaide would ever return here, and that saddened me. But Lexi had made memories. Hopefully some of them had been memories she'd cherish for the rest of her life.

Who knew? Maybe when Lexi was a woman in her late fifties, she'd see that the campground she'd visited when she was a child was for sale. She'd think of me, of my mom, of Elvis, of Denver Twigg, better known as Dorito Man, and she'd feel something stir in her heart.

Maybe she'd buy this campground, and like me forty years before her, she'd arrive full of hopes and dreams, wanting to recapture the happiness of her youth, wanting to create that same happiness for others.

Or not. All the happy memories in the world might never erase the fact that she'd lost her father here.

Their truck vanished from sight and I sighed. There was paperwork to do, the reservations for next week to go over, and the items at the camp store really needed a quick inventory.

But none of that appealed to me at the moment. I had that hollow feeling in my chest, and I knew I needed something to make me feel whole again. I needed something to remind me of the beauty in the world, of the good people who existed right here in my campground and in my town.

"Hike or canoe?" I asked Elvis.

The hound wagged his tail, clearly up for any adventure. That's when I heard the sound of tires on gravel and looked around to see a truck coming into the campground—a familiar truck that towed a trailer with a fishing boat on it.

I waved as Jake drove past toward the boat launch, and made up my mind.

"Canoeing it is," I told Elvis. "And if we're lucky, maybe we'll catch a fish."

* * *

WANT MORE? Sign up for my newsletter and never miss a new release!

The next book in the Reckless Camper Cozy Mystery Series, The Green Rush, is coming soon.

ABOUT THE AUTHOR

Libby Howard lives in a little house in the woods with her sons and two exuberant bloodhounds. She occasionally knits, occasionally bakes, and occasionally manages to do a load of laundry. Most of her writing is done in a bar where she can combine work with people-watching, a decent micro-brew, and a plate of Old Bay wings.

For more information:
libbyhowardbooks.com/

ACKNOWLEDGMENTS

Special thanks to Lyndsey Lewellen for cover design and Kimberly Cannon for editing.

In memory of my mother who was my biggest fan and my partner-in-crime.

CPSIA information can be obtained
at www.ICGtesting.com
Printed in the USA
BVHW081249161222
654329BV00006B/259

9 781952 216589